Demi

Kayleigh Greer

Books by Kayleigh Greer

Femme Fatale Duet

Prudence

Demi

◆

Stand Alone

A Nightingale Without Wings

Book Cover by Kayleigh Greer

Edited by Tonya Bluston

First edition 2023

Instagram: @kayleighgreerauthor

For Kim.

NOTE TO THE READER

This book contains adult material including references to PTSD, sexual assault, child abuse, and graphic depictions of violence. As someone who struggles with my own traumas, I sought to handle these topics with the care and respect they deserve. Thank you for reading.

Prologue

April 2020

Prudence walked steadily down the long stretch of hallway leading to the front office of the prison. Officer Turner—or Gerty, as Prudence had come to affectionately refer to her—walked alongside.

Prudence looked at her briefly, perhaps searching for reassurance.

All these emotions, which she had gone so long without experiencing, sometimes confused her immensely. It was hard to discern what they meant. It was especially confounding when she was afflicted with what felt like joy and anxiety at the same time. How two vastly contradictory feelings could cohabitate within her mind completely eluded her.

Currently, she was able to detect excitement, uncertainty—which flared that all-too-familiar anxiety—and then a final emotion she was not happy to have back.

Fear.

"You alright, Demi?" Gerty asked, nudging her genially. Both she and Vincent had taken to calling her that exclusively. They thought it would be integral to her "healing journey," as Gerty had put it.

Manifesting who you were always meant to be, she had said. Prudence understood and appreciated the sentiment but didn't believe she deserved the name just yet.

The hall was coming to an end. The blazing fluorescent lights made the bleak white walls and tiles of the floor so bright it was like walking through clouds toward the sun.

"Fine," Prudence replied, though it was a lie. Her insides fought to avoid imploding due to nerves.

Gerty adjusted her belt. Her pink cheeks were pushed up past her face mask, hiding her emerald green eyes as she smiled widely. "I'm so excited for you! It's going to be like a fresh start—kind of."

Prudence nodded, her hands clutching the counter before her at the end of the hall. Another officer peered at her through the window in front of her and Gerty. He rummaged through some paperwork before saying, "Malkin, Prudence?"

Her chest tightened when she heard her surname. She wasn't so sure if this *healing journey* would lead her to a point where the name Malkin didn't elicit a jarring response from the pits of her ravaged soul.

"That is correct," Prudence replied through the speaker.

Beside the window was a receptacle where the officer placed a box. He closed the door and motioned for her to retrieve it from her end. The hatch clanged loudly in her ears as she grabbed it. Printed on the side of the box were her name and inmate number.

"I'm going to unlock the door to your right. When you hear a buzzing sound, you and Officer Turner may go through. There's a restroom on the left for you to change."

Prudence nodded again, then looked toward Gerty as the buzzer went off and she opened the door.

"I'll wait for you while you change," Gerty said. "Vincent should be here in, like, ten minutes."

Prudence clutched the box to her chest, "Ok. Thank you."

In the bathroom, she set the box on the counter and opened the lid. Inside were her purse, her shoes, and the outfit she had worn on the day she turned herself in.

The day she murdered her landlady, Gretchen Hale.

She vividly remembered every puncture and every slice she had inflicted upon Gretchen. How the blood had flowed from her neck like a waterfall of deep crimson. The lilac blouse Gretchen wore had been stained a dark reddish brown.

The clothes in the box, of course, weren't the ones she had worn when she'd murdered Gretchen. Those clothes had blood splatter, sweat, and semen all over them. Now they were in some warehouse where the police stored their crime scene evidence.

Prudence had taken the time to shower as she waited for the police to come. That was the last time she had enjoyed a quality body wash that wasn't fragrance-free and didn't leave her skin dry, stripped of its natural oils.

She lifted the garments out of the box and inhaled deeply to find that they still had traces of that soap.

Rose and shea.

Something bloomed beneath her rib cage at the scent, at the memory—though it was vile. She felt the exhilarating fervor of freedom.

Prudence removed her face mask and set it on the counter beside the box, then stripped her prison uniform away. She slipped the dress from the box over her head and pushed her feet into her boots. It was a simple form-fitting black dress that fell to just above her knees. The coat she pulled on was an amethyst purple.

How I've missed normal clothes.

When she exited the bathroom, looping the mask back over her ears, Gerty gasped at the sight of her.

"Dem, you are so hot!" Gerty said. Prudence was thankful for the mask as she blushed beneath it. She had found an eyeliner pen in her purse and some lipstick. She thought it absurd to put on lipstick when she had to wear a mask, but she relished applying the winged eyeliner she used to wear. Then, looking in the mirror, she let her hair down and fluffed out her curls.

"That's not news, Gerty," Prudence replied genially.

Gerty laughed and pulled Prudence into a tight, warm embrace. Prudence went rigid, not holding Gerty back. She doubted she would ever care for any form of public display of affection, but she'd let her have this one.

Something plumed in her chest again.

Gerty pulled away, tears lining her plump cheeks. "Alright. Vin texted me that he's here. I've got to walk you out to the gate."

Prudence clutched her purse and exhaled long and slow. They started for the door. Once they were outside, the sun glistened over her. Despite the slight chill in the air, her skin warmed to the sun's presence in the most luxurious way.

Almost there.

Gravel crunched beneath their feet as they neared the gate. Her stride quickened as if any minute someone would charge out of the prison after her. To take her back and claim it had been a mistake.

On the other side of the gate she saw a large, broad-shouldered figure inside a truck. His back churned as he opened the door and emerged into that holy sunlight, which cast a glow on his face.

Prudence quickened her pace once more, so close to the gate now. “Vincent!”

He shut the door and walked around the truck, where she took in the full scope of him. He wore a black long-sleeved shirt with the sleeves rolled up to his elbows, revealing his thickly muscled forearms. Dark blue jeans and brown suede boots completed the look.

Gerty gave the signal and the gates opened before her. Prudence’s eyes were locked on Vincent as he opened the passenger-side door for her and stood patiently waiting.

“Behave out there,” Gerty said, pulling Prudence out of her trance. “I’ll come visit you soon, if that’s ok?”

A flicker of a smile curled the ends of Prudence’s lips beneath the mask. “Of course.” her eyes trailed back to Vincent. “Goodbye, Gerty.”

Prudence walked through the gate toward Vincent’s truck. She approached him, staring into his eyes and over his face, admiring the beard that curled out from under his mask. She’d thought about it for days now. Her eyes glazed over as she slipped into the truck and they drove away.

She was free.

Chapter 1

May 1993

There was a pointed chill in the air as the last dregs of winter withered in spring's germinating wake. Long stretches of fields along Interstate 287 were generously freckled with fragrant daffodils—waves of butter yellow and white petals. When she was a child, Lara had always wondered how something that smelled so sweet could be so toxic. Their family dog, Bosco, had gotten terribly ill after eating a few from their lawn. His vomit was speckled yellow and green submerged in foamy bile.

She never knew whether he survived it.

Her bare feet propped up on the dashboard, Lara peeked over at Sam from past her cherry-red, cat-eye-framed sunglasses. When he didn't immediately look her way, she slowly pulled her lollipop from between her lips and twirled it over the tip of her tongue.

Look at me, you bastard.

Sam's eyes remained fixed on the road ahead. Lara huffed and resumed watching the daffodils fly by in a blur. He was too eager about the *new girl* to even bother noticing her. In fact, all through this last year together, he had seemed to be losing interest. Perhaps she had exceeded her prime in his eyes.

Sixteen was starting to look too old.

Lara pushed her sunglasses over her brow and wrapped her arms around her legs, pulling her knees farther into her chest. Only a few years ago, he had wanted *her* just as badly, and now here he was excited about a *baby*. When she asked him, he swore the baby wasn't for his pleasure. Said she was going to be like their daughter. But Lara didn't want a baby. She wanted it to be just the two of them, forever and ever, like he promised. She wasn't at all interested in being a mom and didn't even like caring for baby dolls when she was younger.

But she wanted Sam.

Above all else, she wanted him and wanted to make him happy. If this was what it took, then fuck it. Lara wiped her teary eyes over her bare knees and turned to look at Sam again, her sunglasses sliding back over her red-rimmed eyes. As he drove, she watched him, admiring everything about him, from the wave in his hair to his clean-shaven chin.

Yeah, she'd do anything for Sam.

"How long before we're there?" Lara asked, her words slightly muffled as they crawled over her lollipop.

"Another hour, doll."

Lara sighed loudly, exclaiming her boredom, and sat up straight in her seat. "I'm starving! Could we stop for a snack? Pleeease?"

"No can do. Ramona gave us a very tight window to pick up the girl. Pulling over now would set us back too much. Besides, you've got that sucker to hold you over."

Lara pulled out the lollipop and frowned at it. Twisting it around between her index finger and thumb, she saw where bits of the candy were wearing thin, revealing the pink bubble gum inside.

Her eyes rolled back to Sam and then down to his lap. "I could use something else to suck on."

The side of Sam's mouth hitched up in a smirk. "Road head at eighty miles per hour is very deadly, doll."

Lara discarded the lollipop in the car's ashtray and leaned over the center console. Her shiny baby blue fingernails ticked over the buckle of his belt as she curled her tongue out the side of her mouth. But Sam didn't budge, not a fraction of an inch, to allow her easy access to what she desired between his legs.

Taking one hand off the wheel, he plucked her fingers from his belt and settled them back on her side of the car. "Be a good girl."

Lara huffed again, slouching back into her seat and crossing her arms, "Since when did you want me to be a good girl?"

"Since we became parents," Sam replied, sparing her a glance. "What should we name her?"

"She's already got a name, doesn't she?" Lara stubbornly looked out the window.

Sam shrugged, his expression serene. "Sure, but she can't keep it. That would make it too easy for anyone who came looking for her."

Lara shrugged defiantly, uninterested in humoring him if he wasn't going to humor her. Though she couldn't help but start racking her brain for different names he might like. He wouldn't care for anything too common. He had complained enough about how average his own name was, so something simple like Emily or Mary wouldn't do. Perhaps he'd favor a name like Genevieve or Josephine or...

“Prudence,” she said. Her eager eyes clicked back over to him, hoping for a satisfied nod.

To her delight, Sam smiled, “Hmm, I like that. Prudence it is.”

CHAPTER 2

April 2020

"Would you mind if I removed my mask?" Prudence asked, causing Vincent's eyes to snap back onto the road. She noticed him unabashedly stare at her from the corner of her eye. A thrill tingled through her, its effect given away only by her eyes.

Vincent cleared his throat, eyes fixed on the road ahead now. "You don't have any symptoms, right?"

The prison officials, of course, had mentioned COVID-19 and the symptoms associated with it. Fever, sore throat, coughing, fatigue. To Prudence, they sounded like the same symptoms for anything else from the common cold to the flu aside from the loss of taste and smell. How could a person possibly know early on that COVID wasn't just sinuses? Regardless, the virus was running rampant through the prison and was partially to thank for her restricted early release.

Partially.

Several inmates were being set for early release as a means of freeing up the prison population. The hope was that the reduction in overcrowding would lessen the spread of the virus. To prepare for her release, Prudence had been tested for the virus and come up negative. This wasn't much of a surprise given that she was regularly kept alone and away from the other inmates. Still, for Vincent's sake, she swiftly took an internal assessment of her health and came up clear of symptoms. Her throat wasn't itchy, her mucus had run clear when she'd checked that morning, and she had no fever. She could smell the warm vanilla notes in Vincent's scent and taste the residual mint from her toothpaste.

"No. I feel fine and I tested negative yesterday," she finally said.

"Me too. I think it should be ok."

He seemed nervous, fidgeting in his seat, as she removed the mask and crumpled it up into her fist. She was thrilled that her skin was no longer gaunt and ashen, having regained its suppleness and toasted golden hue. The last time he saw her, she was unhealthy and deflated following everything that had transpired.

The discovery of who she really was.

The blood of Benitez and the other inmates that thickly coated her skin.

Vincent peeled away his mask, his beard puffing out from beneath it, and offered her a small smile. Nerves now welled up from her belly and singed her cheeks. Warmth spread throughout Prudence's chest and between her thighs. Her lashes hung heavy and she bit her bottom lip involuntarily as she looked him over. Her body quickened and her sex throbbed beneath her clenched hands. She pressed her legs together to quell the ache and quickly resumed looking out the window.

She couldn't seduce and use him again.

No matter how deliciously tempting he was or how comforting he felt, he was not that kind of man. The kind of man she sought out to soothe her troublesome inclination was inconsequential, the bond irrelevant, his feelings and intentions meaningless. Vincent was none of those things to her anymore.

What is this resignation? she wondered.

Reverence?

Fear?

Shame?

Maybe it's borne from all of it...

Instead, she sat quietly and pretended not to notice the lustful vamp who tore her apart from the inside, attempting to claw her way out.

"I spoke with Carmina yesterday afternoon about meeting up to get your things," Vincent said, breaking their prolonged silence.

Prudence furrowed her brow. "Carmina?"

"Carmina Rizzo? She was in your file listed as the power of attorney over your affairs?"

Realization struck her like a ton of bricks. He was talking about Ms. Rizzo, her boss from the firm. Without any family or friends, Prudence had no one else to put down when she was arrested. No one else she trusted—not that she trusted Ms. Rizzo very much as it was.

"Of course. Thank you."

Suddenly, talking was very difficult. Her throat seized and her chest tightened with the pressure of concealing her primitive desires. She hadn't felt even the slightest inkling of her affliction arise until a few days ago. For the last several months, she had been speaking to a therapist, with whom her sessions would remain mandatory as a condition of her release. His name was Dr. Osiris Agubulom. He was an older man somewhere between fifty-five and sixty, with dark, rich skin and abating soft eyes magnified by perfectly round spectacles. When she described her affliction to him, he didn't bat an eye, clearly having heard and experienced his fair share of the bizarre and irrational. He gave her a list of coping mechanisms and exercises for when the feelings inevitably resurfaced. Number one on the list was to breathe.

So she sat quietly, focusing on a drop of moisture that had adhered to her window, and breathed.

◆

Vincent fished his keys out of his pocket. The moment he slid the key into the lock, a dog started howling from the other side of the door. The dog's nails scratched the hardwood floor as he spun with the excitement of knowing his person was about to come inside.

"Is that Broccoli?" Prudence asked, clenching the hem of her coat.

"The one and only!" Vincent said, opening the door with a smile.

Broccoli spun faster and faster as they walked inside and shut the door. His entire bottom shook for lack of a long tail, and he whined up at them. Prudence looked down at the dog for a moment before bending down and offering her hand to him. He lapped away at her fingers and palm before nudging his head into her hand, initiating pets. She obliged, rubbing her thumb between his eyes and scratching the area beneath his chin.

"Usually when he meets new people he's a little standoffish. He's a jealous little shit." Prudence gazed up at Vincent. A hunger swept over her expression at the sight of him, "He must see something good in you," Vincent added.

Unlikely. There's too much darkness inside me.

Prudence's eyes fell to the ground, heavy with melancholy, and Broccoli scampered away to his water dish, evidently parched from all the excitement. Vincent scooped his finger beneath her chin and brought her face to meet his, "There *is* good in you, Demi. I can see it too."

The way her birth name dripped from his tongue like honey doused her heart and filled her with a roaring flame. Its warmth blistered the heavy sadness burrowed deep within her chest.

He caressed her jaw line with his fingertips and said, "Come on, let me show you around."

His apartment was tiny. The kitchen—or kitchenette, rather—took up the space of a corner to the left of the front door. A small refrigerator was pressed against the wall, and beside it was a sliver of counter beside a single sink. A narrow island served as a divider between the kitchen and living room area, where a brown sectional sat in the middle of the floor facing a TV. The room also contained shelves lined with books and movies. They were topped with a pair of ivies whose stems of luscious leaves trailed near the ground.

A small two-seater table was tucked in the corner opposite the kitchen. Near it was a pair of French doors leading to what she presumed was his bedroom. He walked her to his room, which was pitch black except for the light that seeped in from behind them. Vincent continued through the darkness with the confidence of someone very familiar with their surroundings and pulled the blackout curtains apart. A stream of gold light rushed into the room, eating away at all the pockets of shadow. Prudence could now see his neatly made bed, on which sat several shopping bags.

"You can have the room, of course, so do whatever you need to make it your own. I'll crash on the couch," he told her, walking up to the bed and taking a seat.

"No, Vincent, I can't kick you out of your own room."

He patted the bed for her to sit beside him. "My mom would strangle me if I let a woman sleep on the couch."

Prudence sat beside him and pressed her legs firmly together, pretending that the image of his naked body didn't flash through her mind as her brain formed fantasies of all that he could do to her on this bed.

With a great deal of effort, she kept her expression impassive.

Vincent handed her the first of the bags. "I got you a few things to hopefully help you feel at home."

She took the bag and thanked him. Inside she found rose-scented everything: body wash, lotion, shampoo and conditioner, perfume. A small smile tugged at the corner of her mouth. During one of their many phone conversations, she had told him that rose was her favorite fragrance.

He is so thoughtful.

From the other bags, she pulled out a pink loofah, a matching exfoliating cloth, a nail brush, a scalp scrubber, a pumice stone, a toothbrush, toothpaste, floss, and mouthwash. Her throat grew tight.

"Oh, and this." Vincent sat up to retrieve his wallet from his back pocket and handed her a card. "It's from my mom."

Prudence took the card and ran her thumb over it. Her palms grew sweaty and her brows creased as she looked up at him in surprise at the gift she had received from a woman she had never met.

He smirked. "I told her how much you like to read. She got that gift card so you could order a few books. There's fifty dollars on it, I think."

Prudence held it to her chest and a newly familiar presence of tears welled up in her eyes. She couldn't remember the last time she had received a gift, let alone so many.

"I'm sorry if this is too much." Vincent pushed the gifts back on the bed and embraced her. "I should have waited."

She sniffed back a shaking breath and nuzzled into his shoulder. "It's all very thoughtful. Really… thank you."

He pulled back, his arm still looped around her shoulders. "How do you feel?"

Prudence paused, taking an internal assessment and giving names to all the foreign emotions racking her nervous system. "Um… I feel sad. Undeserving. And yet… I feel joy. Gratitude."

Broccoli's nails clicked against the floor as he trotted into the room, his belly full of food and water. He circled their feet and then curled up on the floor between them. The dog's voice squeaked as a ferocious yawn overtook him.

Joy shined more brightly in her eyes as she looked down at the jovial pup. "I'd like to thank her. Do your mother and father live nearby? "

Vincent visibly deflated, removing his arm from around her and rubbing his hands together, though a soft smile remained on his lips. "Yeah, she does."

"Did I say something wrong?" Prudence asked. The warmth from his arm on her shoulders cooled rapidly, sending a shiver down her spine.

"No, you didn't say anything wrong. When you said 'mother *and* father,' it felt like I had returned to a time when my dad was still here. He died a few years ago... so it's just my mom."

Sadness swelled within her again. *Damn these fucking ludicrous, arbitrary emotions.*

She straightened her spine, pinching the sorrow between each vertebra that forced her to slouch. "I'm sorry for your loss."

Vincent nodded and swiftly changed the subject. "Are you hungry?"

Chapter 3

She was so beautiful.

Earlier that day, Vincent had hardly been able to take his eyes off Demi to focus on the road ahead. He had affectionately scoured every inch of her. She had sat quietly with her hands folded in her lap, gazing out the window at the steadily melting snow lining both sides of the road. He had never seen her in anything but her prison garments. Now, wearing a coat and a tight black dress that hugged her curves, she was like a different person.

The same day he saw her in the psych ward, after Benitez's funeral, he had resigned from his position at the prison. Vincent couldn't continue to work there knowing he would be kept from seeing her, so he'd decided to apply at the Criminal Investigation Division. When he was fresh out of college, he had worked a few years as a police officer patrolling the streets of Portland. However, once the burnout started setting in from the politics of the job, Gallagher had convinced Vincent to join him at the prison. Now, after the work he had put into uncovering Prudence's true identity, he was inspired to try his hand at investigating.

Not long after this, the pandemic hit and he was prohibited from seeing her altogether, though he spoke with her over the phone several times a week. Brocc was driving him nuts, and her call was all he looked forward to as he quarantined alone in his apartment, sifting through cold case files that he was tasked with researching remotely.

Now, after six long months, here she was in his apartment, looking healthier than he'd ever seen her. Demi's skin glowed and her unbound curls bounced with every step. He wanted so badly to touch her soft hair, to caress the back of her neck as he ran his fingers up through the silky strands.

In a heated pan, Vincent tossed a tablespoon of butter, then spread it around as it melted rapidly beneath his spoon. Demi was in the bathroom taking a shower as he cooked dinner so she could eat before her virtual session with her therapist. Chicken and lemon potatoes was the go-to quick dinner that his mom had taught him to cook when he was a kid.

He hoped it would be as comforting for Demi as it was for him.

Vincent could plainly see that she was struggling. There was no denying the glazed look in her eyes that had drawn him in the first time or the way her chest shuddered on a breath. He hoped she didn't feel uncomfortable—and that he wasn't the one who was causing her discomfort.

For the dozenth time, Vincent's phone buzzed on the counter, and he picked it up to see who it was now. First it had been Gerty reaching out to make sure Demi was ok. Then it had been Carmina Rizzo responding to his message and agreeing to meet at the end of the week. Last was his mom checking in on him. Though she was trying to be open minded about Demi, she couldn't shake the fear elicited by the fact that a convicted murderer was living with her one and only son. He understood her reservations, of course, as they were perfectly reasonable. However, he knew Demi. He knew she would never hurt him.

```
4:38 pm

Gallagher: Hey Vin. You and Prue ok?
Gallagher: Sorry. Demi*
Vincent: So far so good. Thanks for checking
in, man. Anything new on Benitez's case?
Gallagher: Nah. It's been pretty quiet. Drinks
at your place tomorrow night?
Vincent: See you then.
```

He slid his phone into his back pocket and pulled the boiling pot of potatoes off the burner to strain the water. Steam billowed from the sink as he poured the scalding liquid down the drain.

Since the pandemic hit, he hadn't seen much of his friend Joe Gallagher. Gallagher had contracted COVID early on and had been hospitalized for a week because of it. Only recently had he been able to return to work, thankfully without any debilitating lasting symptoms. Vincent had read about much worse outcomes for several hundreds of thousands of people across the United States. When he first learned that Gallagher was sick, he was devastated, knowing it could be a death sentence for his best friend. Not being able to visit him in the hospital only made things worse.

As Vincent moved on to prepare the chicken, he felt a comforting sense of deep gratitude that his friend was still around.

◆

Prudence stepped out of the shower and wrapped herself in a clean towel that Vincent had set out on the counter. Her skin vibrated with the thrill of being clean and the scent of roses from her gifted products. She had thoroughly bathed herself in a way she hadn't been able to in almost a year, scrubbing off every bit of the dry residue left behind by the prison soap. She stripped the smell of her cell from her hair and, with her nail brush, removed the grime from underneath her fingernails. Now wrapped in a plush, warm towel, she felt brand new and, despite the persistent ache in her core, relaxed.

Until they got her clothes and other belongings from Ms. Rizzo, Vincent had offered her anything in his wardrobe that she'd like to borrow. She opened his drawers and pulled out a pair of boxer briefs and a plain white T-shirt.

She laid the clothes onto the bed and let the towel fall to her feet. She ignored her brain's immediate hope that Vincent would walk in on her completely naked and bent over, easily accessible from the back. Pushing the thoughts down, Prudence generously lathered her skin in the florally robust fragrance of her lotion. Once dressed, she stood before the partially fogged-up mirror and looked at herself. Running her hands over her neck and chest in the crisp, clean shirt, which was deeply imbued with his scent, she wondered what he would think of her in his clothes.

Would he think she was beautiful?

Would he be aroused by the way her nipples pressed against the shirt? Their dark areolas showed through the white fabric. Her chest rose and fell with her shallow breaths as the ache built up within her. She imagined her fingers were his as they trailed from her breasts, down her stomach, and to the apex of her thighs. She was running her thumb over her clit through the fabric of the boxers when a knock on the bedroom door startled her.

"Can I come in?" Vincent asked from the other side of the door.

Only if you promise to take me now.

"Yes. Yes, you may." Her voice cracked over the words as embarrassment heated the tips of her ears.

He opened the door and stepped inside. "Ready to eat?"

"I am." She left the bathroom, avoiding his gaze as she ran her fingers through her damp hair, though it didn't matter. She could feel his eyes burning into her skin as he watched her.

Vincent cleared his throat and extended his hand. "Come on, I've set the table."

Prudence walked past him to the table just outside the bedroom, steering clear of his touch for fear that she would combust. Vincent scratched the back of his neck and followed, taking his seat across from her at the table.

"How was your shower?" he asked, sinking his teeth into his first bite. Prudence looked down at the plate he had fixed for her, admiring the effort he must have put into the meal. However, her appetite for food was nonexistent.

A typical symptom of her affliction.

She lifted her fork and forced herself to take a bite for him. Her stomach rolled happily in the presence of food regardless of her mind's protests.

"It was marvelous. I hadn't realized how much I'd missed decent water pressure," she replied.

"Yeah, the showers in prison are pretty bad."

Her mind instantly went back to the time he'd fucked her in the solitary showers months ago. His long, hard cock, how it had stretched her. She dabbed her brow with her napkin and Vincent took a sip of water as he watched her reluctantly take another bite.

"I'm glad you're here," he said.

She looked up at him, bewilderment etched in her expression. "I am too. It just—well it still feels very much like a dream."

Vincent reached across the table and squeezed her hand. Prudence froze beneath his touch. The calluses of his palms scraped against her skin and her body hummed in response. "I think they made the right choice. Someone like you didn't deserve to be in prison."

A pang of guilt dissipated the ache substantially. "I hope you're right."

"Maybe after your therapy session we can order you a few books with your gift card," Vincent said, squeezing her hand before resuming his dinner.

Prudence flexed the hand he released and slid it into her lap. She took another bite and offered him a small smile.

Hopefully, this time the books will pose a decent enough distraction.

"Gallagher will be coming by tomorrow evening to hang out with me for a little while and have a few beers. I hope you don't mind?" Vincent said, scooping both potato and chicken into his mouth.

Prudence remembered Gallagher. He was kind. It didn't bother her that he would be coming, but strangely enough, the idea of his impending presence did not elicit any physical response. Not that any and every person set her urges aflame, but he was not an unattractive man in his own right. No, it was only Vincent whom she was drawn to. As she slowly looked up at him from her plate, her body warmed at the sight of his beard, which had once tickled her in her most sensitive of places.

It was Vincent for whom her mind and body were always searching.

"I don't drink," Prudence finally responded, noticing how the silence began to weigh the air around them.

"That's ok. You're not obligated to drink with us. But if you start to feel uncomfortable, just let me know." Vincent smiled at her. "Oh, and Carmina said she was free Sunday to get your things."

Prudence nodded and reluctantly took another bite. She couldn't deny that she felt better after having eaten, but something inside was repelled by it. She pushed the troublesome feeling down and reminded herself that while her wants and needs did not always align, it was her needs that must now take precedence.

She watched Vincent in silence and gaped at the way his throat bobbed as he drank from his glass of water. She took in the crease in his brow, the way he licked the droplets from his lips.

My needs...

CHAPTER 4

After getting her set up in the room on his laptop, Vincent closed Prudence inside to give her privacy during her session. On the screen, she watched as the video chat app rang Dr. Osiris Agubulom. In the bottom right-hand corner, she saw her own image in a small box. She scooped a stray curl behind her ear just as Osiris accepted the call. His image took over the larger portion of the screen, a wide toothy smile on his face.

"Good evening, Prudence," he said in his baritone voice that wove around a Nigerian accent. He appeared to be seated at his desk, wearing a tan blazer and an orange tie. His spectacles reflected the light of his own screen, which displayed her image.

"Good evening, Osiris."

His eyes searched her face as they always did, studying her like the insightful scholar he was. "You are looking well. How is freedom treating you?"

Prudence's spine was perfectly straight as she sat with her legs crossed on the bed. Her hands fidgeted in her lap. "I'm well."

He nodded, "Inshallah. How is Vincent? Are you at ease in his home?"

"Good and yes, it's quaint."

Osiris nodded again, his almond-shaped eyes narrowing slightly. "Has your anxiety continued?"

Her face remained impassive. In the past, she had been unwilling to discuss anything or accept any help from doctors or therapists and was quite obstinate—if not hostile—toward them. But things were different now. If she wanted to become who she was always meant to be, if she wanted to make Vincent proud and feel whole enough to reach out to her birth parents, she had to try.

"Slightly," she replied. "I feel like I didn't deserve this second chance now that I have it."

"Because of what you did to Gretchen?"

And Flor Juarez, and Anita Bell, and Elanor Johnson, and Mari Velasco... but he didn't know about them, nor could he.

Prudence bowed her head, unable to look into his eyes as she was forced to leave them out of their discussions yet again. "Yes. At times I think they made a mistake."

"Do you plan on hurting anyone else?" he asked.

"No." She shook her head vehemently. "Never again. I do worry about my impulses, how strong they can be, but that can no longer be who I am. They can no longer consume me."

Osiris smiled reassuringly. "Then we won't let them, now will we?"

She nodded, the corner of her mouth ticking up slightly in response.

"When last we spoke," he continued, " you expressed that you felt bad for not knowing that Gretchen had had a family, for not truly knowing her."

Prudence nodded.

"I took it upon myself to gather information about her on your behalf should you like to learn about her." Her stomach sank and her expression contorted. "Now, what I have found is nothing too personal, and I will not require you to speak with the family, as that is a choice for them to make as well. However, if you are interested in learning about her, I'll gladly share with you what I have found."

She considered his offer for a moment, terrified that what she learned would only deepen her guilt. Everyone around her extolled the importance of being open to accountability. She understood that thorough accountability could be achieved only by complete transparency and understanding the full scope of her crimes. This undoubtedly included her victims and who they were.

"Yes, I would."

Osiris offered a reassuring smile and, in a soothing, velvety tone, reminded her to breathe. Then he shared his screen, where he read directly from Gretchen's obituary.

Gretchen Hale
9/27/1961-12/15/2018

She is survived by her two sons Alan Hale Jr. and John Hale-Billafuerte. Grandchildren Mandy Hale, Lynnette Hale, Armand Hale-Billafuerte, and Rosaline Hale-Billafuerte. Sister Belinda Sabinske and brother Victor Sabinske.

She is preceded in death by her husband Alan Hale Sr., her parents Michael and Jacquelyn Sabinske, and her brother John Sabinske.

He scrolled down past the obituary, where a slew of family photographs littered the screen. She immediately recognized Gretchen in every photo, even those that depicted her younger than she had been when Prudence took her life. And she was hit again with those many eyes, noses, and hair textures that Gretchen and her family shared. Prudence recognized one of her sons as the man who had spoken out during her trial, tears in his heavy, red-rimmed eyes.

"Is the one wearing yellow in this photo Alan or John?" she asked.

Osiris squinted at the photo and said, "That is John. Beside him is his husband Antonio and their children Armand and Rosaline."

Tears welled up in her eyes. How she would have cherished having parents who loved her like Armand and Rosaline's parents seemed to do. To have had a grandmother who doted on her like Gretchen must have doted on them.

I took her from those children.

Prudence cleared her throat and wiped her tears away with the back of her hand, trying to remember to breathe as he proceeded to scroll.

"Here you will see Gretchen with her late husband Alan when they purchased the apartment building that you lived in. According to their tenants over the years, they were exceptional landlords. Very kind and communicative."

Seeing the building again sent a chill over her arms.

"This photo shows Gretchen at a town hall meeting. Evidently, she attended them frequently in hopes of bettering her community. Here she is pictured with her beloved dog, Cooper. Alan Jr. and his wife Sonia now have him."

A bubble swelled in her throat and she covered her mouth to inhibit any cry that tried to escape.

Osiris paused when he noticed her squirm. “We can stop there if you like.”

She exhaled a breath that she hadn’t realized was trapped in her chest. Panting, she nodded in agreement.

He disabled the screen sharing and adjusted his spectacles. “What was going through your mind as I showed you these photos?”

Every fiber in Prudence’s being begged her to stay silent. Her mind screamed excruciatingly loud, telling her to say nothing, reveal *nothing*.

I have to try.

“Um.” Her voice cracked and sweat beaded on her brow. “How—how much I long for an anesthetic. To feel... nothing again.”

Osiris remained quiet and wholly focused on her, leaving the floor open for her to speak.

“I miss the numbness, the indifference. I miss when I could go weeks, even months, at a time between having to deal with these *insufferable*, idiotic feelings. I hate how much guilt I feel. I hate the jealousy I feel for not being dead and six feet under like her. I want my anxiety to die, I want my sorrow to disappear. I want my rage to burn brighter than a supernova and in the cavity of its destruction have it fizzle out into irrevocable obscurity!” Her face was drenched in hot tears and her body quaked beneath the strain. “I want to feel numb.”

Prudence’s chest loosened and she could finally breathe more fluidly. The heat in her skin evaporated, replaced with a coolness that calmed her nervous system. Confused by her body's reaction, she furrowed her brow and glanced up at Osiris for guidance.

He smiled that knowing, toothy grin of his. "It is a wonder what letting it all out can do for our sanity, is it not?"

His chuckle in response to her relaxed sigh was infectious, filling her with warmth.

Was this what it felt like to have a father figure who cared?

This comfort and support, was this how a genuine connection outside the confines of romanticism was supposed to feel?

"The only way we can avoid becoming slaves to our emotions, Prudence, is by facing them. Feeling them and effectively moving through them. There is no way over or around them, no matter how high or far you go."

CHAPTER 5

December 2013

Prudence retrieved her buzzing phone from the front pocket of her duffle bag as she made her way inside the gym for her first kickboxing lesson. The gymnasium's chill, which bit at the nape of her neck, matched that of the air outside. However, she knew the sensation wouldn't last. When she trained, she trained hard. No matter how many fans there were, or how low the AC was set, her body warmed up when she really got going. Prudence was heavy into cardio—treadmill, Stairmaster, cycling classes, aerobics, you name it.

But she had never tried contact sports before.

She was too afraid that the rage, which simmered beneath her skin at all times, would compel her to do irreversible damage to her opponent. After years on the track team through high school and college her body became accustom to rigorous training and even though she took her athletic career no further than that, she found it helped her tremendously in other ways. It became clear to her, however, that the hours-long runs in the morning and the incessant masturbating at night weren't going to cut it with this particular inclination. She'd need to step out of the bounds of her comfort to quell the beast within.

Checking her screen, she saw a notification from one of the various dating apps she frequented. It was a message from a guy she was going back and forth on meeting up with. His generic, flimsy "Good Morning, Beautiful" message at 11:18 am made her eyes roll.

If this class doesn't go well, we'll link up, Prudence decided before shoving her phone back into the pocket without responding.

Once inside, she showed her voucher to the man at the front desk and then proceeded to warm up. Only half a dozen others had arrived, but more were sure to come over the next several minutes. She couldn't be late to anything even if she tried, usually showing up well before she needed to.

Sinking into her stretch, Prudence reached for her left foot, pulling on the taut tendons of her hamstrings. She retracted after a twenty count and reached for her opposite foot. As she did, a memory flashed through her mind—herself lodging a crowbar through her mother's eye. She felt the sensation of blood, exhilaratingly warm, freckle her skin. Prudence gasped and her eyes shot open as they frantically scanned the room.

This was bad.

Very bad.

Images of her parents' murder overcame her only when her inclinations were at their absolute worst. The memories didn't scare her. Much to the contrary, they excited her. Prudence felt her skin tingle at the idea of the blood of someone whose life she had taken spilling over her flesh. She remembered how her heart had leaped in her chest at the freedom that came with driving the curved end of that rusted crowbar into her father's temple. How his arms had reached for her aimlessly as he ran their car into the highway median. A smile had spread across her adolescent face even as their car flipped and she was rendered unconscious.

No. That's enough.

Prudence shook her head, clearing it of sinister thoughts, and rose to her feet when the instructor entered the room. The instructor was a brunette with toned muscles, wearing athletic shorts and a tank top featuring the gym's logo.

"Afternoon, ladies!" she chirped loudly into the headset microphone that sent her voice soaring through the room. "I'm Marybel, your instructor. Welcome to our Intro to Kickboxing course!"

Prudence clapped along with the other women in the room. She was painfully self-aware, trying her best to remain impassive to ensure she came off as normal as possible. She had trouble hearing the instructor through her own mounting internal tension. It was like she was submerged underwater, as the delayed words that reached her ears were warped and practically indiscernible.

Just watch and follow along, Prue.

Focusing on the instructor, Prudence watched Marybel go through the motions of their first set before taking her fighting position and emulating the steps along with the rest of the class.

Left hook, right hook, kick.

Left hook, right hook, kick.

Left hook, right hook, kick.

They completed the set at twenty reps, but the water in Prudence's ears did not subside. Still she watched as Marybel demonstrated the next set.

Right hook, uppercut left.

Right hook, uppercut left.

Right hook, uppercut left.

Prudence's heart was racing, and she knew it wasn't from the sets. They had only just started and it took quite a deal more to get her heart rate up past ninety beats per minute. No, she was spiraling.

Flutter jumps.

Flutter jumps.

Flutter jumps.

She tripped over her own foot and almost fell into the woman beside her. Her legs were shaking, but she had to keep going.

"Excuse me," she said to the woman before falling back into step. Her head was swimming, her brain sloshing between her ears, hitting the cranial wall on either side.

Fuck, this is bad.

"Keep going, ladies!" Marybel called through the sloshing in Prudence's ears. The instructor stood at the front of the class, effortlessly skipping through her flutter jumps. Then the set ended and Prudence just barely made out the words "practice" and "your partner."

Was she supposed to find a partner?

Were they going to fight each other?

She didn't understand until she saw several striking pads being passed around. They were to trade off practicing the hooks, uppercuts, and kicks they had just learned.

Her father's bloodied temple flashed through her mind.

Oh god, no.

Her mother's eye oozed blood over the rusted crowbar.

I've got to get out of here.

Prudence turned to evacuate, bumping into the same woman she had almost tripped over. She held a pair of striking pads.

"Hey, are you ok?" she asked, appearing genuinely concerned.

Prudence looked her in the eyes. In one moment, the woman's throat was slit, her eyes rolling into the back of her head, the bloodied knife in Prudence's right hand. Then, in the next moment, the woman was fine. Prudence's heart leaped into her throat. She quickly gathered her things and exited the building at a full-speed sprint.

Adjusting the bodice of her dress, Prudence leaned into the bathroom mirror, assessing her appearance. Once she'd made it home, she'd forced herself under a cold shower that froze her every nerve, stripping her mind of the thoughts that had plagued her so fiercely at the gym.

She didn't feel better, but she was calm.

Prudence fluffed her hair and threw her phone into her purse after a quick "on my way" text to her hook-up for the evening. She had just put her hand on the front doorknob when a knock sounded from the other ride. Prudence furrowed her brow. She wasn't expecting company. Cautiously, she unlocked and then opened the door to find Mr. Travis standing behind it. He had been a teacher of hers at St. Joan's Juvenile Detention Center.

The teacher she had fucked when she was fourteen years old.

"Hey, Prue," he said, running his fingers through his honey-blond hair. "It's been a long time."

Chapter 6

April 2020

To Prudence's great surprise, sleep found her fast while she was wrapped in Vincent's bedding on her first night of freedom. The vanilla musk notes in his scent lulled her to sleep with very little difficulty despite the raging desires that wreaked havoc on her internally. She had never been soothed by another person like this.

She took in a deep breath, filling her lungs with life, pulling the comforter into herself. Its soft fabric caressed her cheek. She wished it had been Vincent's callused palm instead. Vincent had slept on the couch, as promised, with Broccoli curled up on the floor beside him. It was as if the dog also wished to give Prudence her privacy and space.

So many sensations rushed through her veins, most of which she could not catch to study their meaning. However, one shined clear and bright: safety. Vincent and everything surrounding him made her feel safe.

With a tug, she freed herself from beneath the mound of blankets and got out of bed. Her body stiffened and creaked as she made her way to the bathroom to straighten up. Prudence washed her face, then used her wet hands to calm the frizz in her hair, her curls cooperated nicely, and then brushed her teeth. Her skin and hair still smelled clean and fragrant and soft to the touch even hours after her first groundbreaking shower outside the prison walls. Very few things made her feel quite as good as being thoroughly clean.

A knock sounded on the bedroom door. "Demi, are you up?" Vincent asked, his tone soft and circumspect, certainly in case she was not yet awake.

Her body shamelessly responded to his presence. Her nipples hardened and her arousal pooled between her thighs. Prudence promptly shook it away as best as she could before rinsing her toothbrush and taking a swig of water from her tumbler. "Yes, please come in."

The door slowly opened and Vincent appeared from behind it. His shirt was wrinkled and his hair was in complete disarray. Even his beard was smashed on one side. A small smile threatened to creep across Prudence's face.

He oozes eroticism.

He squinted at her through sleep-rimmed eyes and wished her good morning with a toothy smile. "Sorry to bother you so early. A small apartment means one bathroom."

"You're alright," Prudence said, crossing her arms over her budding nipples and moving aside for him to pass. Vincent shut the door behind him and as he relieved himself, he called out, "How did you sleep?"

She grimaced, unaccustomed to someone being comfortable with conversing while they urinated. Was he normally that comfortable or was he just comfortable with her?

Deep down, in a long-forgotten well of her humanity, she hoped it was the latter.

"Very well, thank you." Her belly knotted with nerves. "A—And you?"

He flushed the toilet and re-emerged into the room. "Oh yeah, like a baby." He carried on to the sink and washed his hands. As tall as he was in comparison to the e. "I'm about to get dressed for a run. Care to join me?"

Yes, a run would be monumentally helpful in her current state. Prudence looked over at him only to meet his gaze reflected in the mirror. She blushed, to her dismay, and nodded before casting her eyes down to her feet.

"Great!" He shook his hands, causing droplets of water to fleck the sink, before heading back to the door. "I'll walk Brocc really quick before we head out."

"You don't take him on your runs?" Prudence asked.

"With those stubby legs? Nah, he can't keep up with me. But something tells me you can." When Vincent winked at her, Prudence's eyes fluttered inadvertently as her core melted in response. He must have been referring to her endless jogging in circles in her solitary cell. It hadn't done her much good then, but she'd be damned if she didn't try.

Vincent pointed to the dresser. "Bottom drawer. I have some sweats with a drawstring that you can adjust if you need to so they stay up while we run."

◆

The early-morning Portland breeze at the onset of spring was still fairly cold thanks to their location right off the coast. It quite literally sliced through their clothes as Vincent and Demi ran down the streets of downtown. Vincent loved the chill. In fact, he thrived in it. The muscles in his legs burned so good against the icy current and propelled him forward, faster and harder. He was ecstatic at how well Demi kept up alongside him. He wore one of his wireless earbuds and she wore the other as they listened to a training playlist of his.

"Flames" by Tedy filled their ears at that moment. To Vincent, this felt ironic considering the frigid temperatures—though its theme was apt. Just as Tedy sang about the flames he felt, Vincent felt flames lick every spot where Demi's eyes lingered for too long.

He peeked at her as she ran beside him. She wore his clothes—a pair of gray sweats and a bulky sweater. Her curls were bound and stuffed beneath a beanie. Vincent smiled at her rosy nose and cheeks, kissed by the chill in the air.

They cut around a corner, narrowly avoiding a puddle of mostly melted snow on the ground surrounding a fire hydrant. Instinctively, he lunged to catch her should she fall, but Demi leaped over it, landing on the tread of her boots. Vincent felt bad for not having any running shoes she could borrow, but she didn't seem to be deterred. "You holding up ok, Dem?"

"Yes," she replied, a puff of mist emerging from the warmth of her lungs.

They carried on through downtown Portland, rounding the Our Lady of Victory statue in Monumental Square, then running past the art museum. The streets were clear, with not a soul in sight as the city quarantined. Shops were closed left and right, from the haberdashery to the Green Hand Bookshop.

It was like they were the last two souls on Earth.

When they came upon State Street, Vincent slowed to a stop to catch his breath. "We'll head back from here."

"Why?" Demi asked, panting. "Why not go farther?"

With his hands on his knees, Vincent looked back over his shoulder past State Street, then back at her. "Farther!" He laughed. "Dem, you can't be serious. We just ran three miles and still have to make it back."

Demi shuffled her feet, her chest rising and falling as her breath struggled to catch up. She seemed to be agitated, maybe even anxious. He watched her kick at a rock as he straightened back up.

"Of course. You're right. We should turn back," she said.

Vincent walked up to her, her gaze conflicted as she averted her eyes, and rested his hand on her shoulder. "No, it's just me. You've got me beat in endurance by a *long* fucking shot."

Demi was statue-like beneath his touch and her face flushed, the rosiness intensifying. She gazed up at him through her curtain of lashes and said, "I can help you work on that."

He gulped. Through the look in her alluring eyes, Vincent could tell that there was something much more salacious behind that remark.

Just as they were ready to take off back home, Vincent's phone buzzed in his pocket and a voice sounded through the earbuds: "Phone call from *Gertrude Turner*. Answer it?"

He tapped his bud to answer. "Hello?"

"Vin!" Gerty shrieked through the receiver, Demi and Vincent cringed. "Don't you know that, until she gets one of her own, this is Demi's phone?"

"I'm here, Gerty," Demi said. "How are you?"

"Demi! I'm good now that I can hear your sweet angel voice again!"

Demi smiled—a rare sight that Vincent was pleased to witness.

"It's only been a day," she reminded Gerty.

"Twenty-two hours and fifteen minutes, Dem. That's a long time for best friends to go without speaking."

Vincent couldn't help but laugh at that as he led the way back at a light jog. Demi followed suit as Gerty continued.

"Anyway, thanks to all the staff that have been furloughed and the cut hours, it's busy as all *hell* over here. Less hours to do twice the work. It's a travesty, if I'm being honest."

"How many were furloughed?" Vincent asked.

"About a hundred people. Now this is the last time I'll say it, Vin, this is an 'A' 'B' conversation, so 'C' your way out."

He threw his hands up in defense despite her not being able to see him and mimed zipping his mouth shut.

"How are you doing Demi?" Gerty continued.

"I'm ok. Had my session with Osiris yesterday, which was difficult but necessary," Demi replied.

Vincent smiled. Though Demi hadn't shared anything with him after her session, he was glad to know she was willing and open with Gerty. Perhaps her having said this in front of him meant she held the same regard for him as well.

"I don't doubt it. Osiris is a cool guy. He reminds me of Uncle Phil from Fresh Prince. You ever watch that show?"

"No, I don't watch TV, remember?" Demi replied with a softness to her tone.

"Not even as a kid?" Gerty asked, then immediately seemed to regret it. "Oops, forget I asked. Sorry."

Vincent noticed Demi was slightly falling behind in her jog. He slowed to look back at her, but he couldn't read the expression on her face.

"I took no offense to your question, Gerty. I think it just made me... sad," Demi revealed. Vincent's heart sank. "Listen, we have a little under three miles to run back to Vincent's. Can I call you later?"

"Three miles! On purpose? Alright, just don't catch COVID. I'll be coming by to visit in a few days if it's alright with *Dad*," Gerty replied.

Vincent knew immediately that he was this "Dad" she referenced. "Yes, Dad approves," he said.

Gerty giggled. "Ok, bye!"

They continued the remainder of their run in silence. Perhaps it was the chill against his calescent skin, or Demi's sheer presence beside him. Or the fact that it felt as though they were the only people in the world running through this ghost town, but it was peaceful sharing this time with her.

CHAPTER 7

Gallagher knocked on the door a few minutes past 7:30 that evening. Vincent invited him inside and Brocc spun in circles at Joe's feet, whimpering and snorting for head scratches.

"Hey, little buddy! Long time no see, huh!" Gallagher laughed as he scratched between the pup's ears.

"Looks like he missed his uncle," Vincent said, shutting and locking the door behind him. When he turned around, his eyes fell on Demi, who stood quickly from her quiet seat on the couch, book in hand, and started for his bedroom door.

When they got home from their run, she was the first to shower, and straight after hopping out, she offhandedly thanked him for the run, not sparing him a single glance. She had then, for the remainder of the morning and afternoon, buried her face in a book that she had borrowed from his shelf. Vincent hadn't pressed her for conversation, though he desperately wanted to. He had spoken with her only twice, asking if she wanted anything to eat, only for her to deny him both times. She went from opening up to Gerty on the phone to folding in on herself and shutting down. Was it because of him? Was it her desires that he became all too familiar with so many months ago?

He wished she would let him help her feel better.

"Hey, Dem!" Gallagher called out, stopping her in her tracks.

Clutching the book to her chest, with her index finger tucked between the pages to save her place, Demi turned back around and gave him a nod without looking him in the eye.

"You don't have to scurry away. You could join us if you'd like," he told her, setting, on the narrow kitchen counter, a large brown paper bag containing their beers for the evening.

"I would not." Demi's tone was curt, but she softened it with an amiable "thank you" before entering the room as she had initially intended. Once the door shut behind her, both Gallagher and Vincent let out a breath.

"Jesus, man, I thought you said she'd loosened up?" Gallagher said, pulling out a beer for each of them—a stout for Vin and a pilsner for himself—before putting the rest in the fridge.

Using his forearm, Vincent twisted off the bottle cap, then discarded it into the trash bin under the sink. "Well," he began, taking a generous gulp, "she has with me. She just needs time. There's a lot she has to adjust to. Plus she has a virtual session with her therapist in a few minutes, so it's not like she could hang for very long anyway."

Gallagher plopped down on the couch and used his toes to pull off his shoes. "No, I get it. I'm sure she's *extra* sweet on you." He winked.

Vincent crossed his brows. When he realized what Gallagher meant, he shook his head. "No, no. We haven't slept together. In fact, I've been sleeping right there," he said, pointing to the couch with his beer-free hand.

"No fucking way!" Gallagher laughed.

"Keep your voice down, Joe, she can hear. These walls aren't exactly soundproof."

Gallagher's face was riddled with surprise. "I thought you two would have hit the sheets the moment she got here."

"No, it's not like that. Since she's been here, she hasn't initiated it, but after what happened with Benitez, I don't blame her." Vincent took another swig of his beer and pulled a chair from his table so that he could sit across from his best friend. "Anyway, how've you been feeling?"

"Never better. Still have trouble smelling anything, but I don't mind that too much. They test us for COVID daily at work, which forces me to stay on top of it without having to stand in some god-awful line outside a booth just to get tested." Gallagher rolled his bottle between his hands. "Speaking of Benitez, though, a dozen more inmates came forward with allegations against him. It's almost daily now that someone's got a new story to tell."

Vincent adjusted in his seat and took the last swig of his beer. He rose to grab them each another bottle. "You don't believe them?"

"No, I *do* believe them. It's just incredible all the shit that guy did. So much more than we even realized." He shook his head as he accepted the fresh beer from Vincent. "Berkeley, little mousy blonde, she said she couldn't afford a pack of cigarettes at the commissary a while back. She said he promised her a full carton if she gave him something in return..."

Vincent leaned forward, elbows resting on his knees, a look of disgust on his face. "What did he do?"

"He, uh... sodomized her anally with his baton." Gallagher shook his head, then drank down half of his beer.

Vincent swore aloud, fury scorching the lining of his stomach. Even in death, Benitez managed to elicit a greater hatred from him than what he had felt before. He knew the depraved bastard had sex with inmates, which was abhorrent in and of itself, but this was almost too much to stomach.

"There are so many stories like it. He's been accused hundreds of times of rape at this point. Accepting sex in exchange for drugs—coke, meth, opioids. They found out that the fuck had a dealer on speed dial. All of this over the span of more than a decade. Hundreds of claims, not including any inmates no longer at the prison. They're keeping very tight-lipped on everything that's coming to light. Everyone had to sign a non-disclosure agreement to make sure we don't speak to any press about what had been going on." Gallagher looked up at Vincent. "Even with him having killed all those women that night in solitary, they're trying to keep all his other bullshit under wraps. I guess to avoid an even more explosive scandal."

Vincent gulped hard, a painful bubble expanding in his chest.

A week before Demi's release, Vincent had received a phone call from Warden Seifert. It was then that he had learned they'd be letting the deceased Edgar Benitez take the fall for the inmates' lives that Demi had taken. Seifert had told him that it was their best option.

Soon after word got out in the jail that Demi had murdered Benitez, rumors spread about how he had victimized her. Collins, the only surviving inmate in solitary other than Demi herself, was very vocal about how he had tried to rape Demi and that she had done what she had to do. Seifert had told Vincent that once her claim gained traction, inmates' claims against Benitez were being reported in droves.

"She told you he tried to rape her, didn't she?" Seifert had asked him repeatedly throughout their conversation.

Vincent had replied "yes" every time.

"Good, good. Then everyone has their story straight. It's bad enough what happened to those women, Vincent, but even if we were to charge Malkin with their murders, she could countersue for gross negligence, misconduct, injury, and rape from not one but two officers. Not to mention the hundreds, maybe even thousands, of lawsuits for the years' worth of accusations against Benitez should this information get out. Our hands are tied!"

Vincent's heart had stopped. "What do you mean *two* officers?"

Seifert had sighed heavily into the phone. "Vin, you're one of the two. You were in a position of power over her. No matter the nature of your relationship as you see it, it's rape in the eyes of the law. She could take you down too."

Vincent didn't believe for a second that she'd do that to him. The rest, however, he wasn't so sure about. She was smart and she'd never go down without a fight—not when she felt justified in her actions. His thoughts had roamed to her parents' murder.

"We wouldn't survive whatever hellfire she and the other victims have in store. We're going to have to chalk it up to murder due to self-defense and let Benitez take the fall for the others. And I'll need *you* to take her."

"Take her?" Vincent had asked, trying and failing to keep up.

"With COVID spreading rampant, we're obligated to let a number of inmates out on early release. It would be in our best interest to get Malkin out and keep her at a safe distance while we figure all this shit out," Seifert had explained. "Will you take her?"

Of course he would and so he did.

Now, seated across from his best friend, Vincent held a secret he could not share with him after years of transparency. The taste of dishonesty was sour on his tongue. He tried to wash it down with the strong bitter coffee notes in the beer.

Gallagher scoffed. "Demi did everyone a favor by doing him in."

Vincent swirled his empty bottle. "Hey, man, can I get you another beer?"

"Hell yeah, that's what I'm here for!" Gallagher replied, handing Vincent his empty bottle. "You wouldn't happen to have any peanuts, would ya? It'd make it *really* feel like we were back at Gritty's if you did."

Vincent chuckled. "Let me check."

His third beer was sure to make the buzz set in. Plus, with a change in conversation topic, the guilt weighing on his shoulders would dissipate enough for him to enjoy the rest of his evening with Gallagher.

CHAPTER 8

Vincent sat across from Demi at his small two-seater table, thumbing through a news article on his phone. He was actively avoiding a case that he had been tasked with a week ago and instead had taken to distracting himself with anything else.

The case hadn't been cold for long, but like so many other similar cases, there wasn't much to go on. He hated feeling so hopeless knowing how unlikely it was that the victim would be brought to justice. However, that was the nature of the job sometimes.

Not fair and extremely fucked up.

So scroll on mindlessly he did as Demi read a new book she had bought online with the gift card his mother had gotten for her. The whole table shook as she aggressively shifted in her seat, swatting through the pages. Vincent peeked up at her and noticed an intense uneasiness about her expression. Her brows were crossed as she sank her fingers into her curls, pulling and twisting them at their roots. Her leg bounced vigorously like she was ready to explode out of her seat.

"Dem?" he said, but she did not answer. She scrunched up her nose and swatted away another page. He tried again. "Demi?"

"What?" she snapped, not looking up at him from her book. She seemed to be struggling greatly to concentrate, as he watched her eyes scan the same section of the page over and over again.

"Are you not enjoying your book?"

Demi slammed it shut and looked up. Flames sparkled in her irises, then simmered when they fell on him. Her bouncing leg stopped and her body grew still.

"Of course I am," she bit out. "Why would you ask that?"

Vincent pointed to her book, closed beneath her palm. "I guess I just figured if you were, you would have saved your place before shutting it."

Frazzled, she looked down at it, removed her hand, then sifted through the pages to find her place. "I-it's not the book. The book is fine."

"Are you ok?"

"Don't be ridiculous. Of course I am!" she groaned, then shut the book again without finding her place.

Vincent set his phone on the table between them and leaned forward. "You're not fine. You haven't been for days."

Demi turned away from him, though he caught her staring out of the corner of her eye. She sat quietly, simmering in her vexation.

He softened his tone before speaking again. "You've been acting exactly the way you did your first week in solitary. Restless, frustrated... I see the looks you give me. The way you react when I'm around."

She did not respond, though he swore he saw her tremble ever so slightly.

"You need a release, don't you, Demi?"

He watched her avert her eyes and cross her arms. Her chest heaved, causing her breasts to swell beneath the button-up flannel shirt she had borrowed from him. The buttons around her chest strained.

There was no denying her desire.

"I won't use you again, Vincent," she replied, her voice tense.

Vincent's brows crossed. "If I'm offering, you wouldn't be—"

"And more than that, my inclinations are *superficial*. Expelled by meaningless sex with quite literally anybody. Take Benitez for a shining example," she interrupted, her blazing eyes falling on him again. "*You* are not just anybody and... it wouldn't be meaningless."

She was right. It wouldn't be meaningless for him either. Never had been. Something about her, from the moment they met, drew him to her like a bee to a fresh bloom. Part of him always longed for her, desired her, wanted to protect her. They were two divine entities serving one another for a purpose larger than either of them could fathom. For a fulfillment nothing else could satisfy.

Vincent's temple pulsed as he ground his teeth, biting back the urge to jump over the table and take her. His fists clenched. "Do you want me, Demi?"

With a sharp inhale, her lips parted slightly as if readying themselves to allow anything to pass—his lips, his tongue, his cock.

"Yes," she whispered.

"If there were another man here, would your inclination have you wanting him too?" he asked, his gaze fixed on her.

"No." Surprise fed the flame in her eyes, as if this were a new realization for her. "I don't want anyone else."

Vincent smirked, a feral look on his face, and leaned back in his seat. When he let his legs fall open, Demi's gaze fell to his groin, where he knew she could plainly see his equal need for her. He watched her hand slide between her legs. Her lashes hung heavy, drunk with longing.

"Then you wouldn't be using me." His hands rested on either of his muscled thighs, and his cock ached to the point of pain as it pressed against the seam of his zipper. "Now *come* here and take what you want."

Shamelessly and without hesitation, Demi slid out of the chair, her knees hitting the floor, and crawled around the table to him. She ran her hands from his knees to the base of his inner thighs, squeezing at his taut muscles as she did. Vincent's cock throbbed at the sight of the hunger in her eyes. He looked down at her, wholly captivated, as she undid the button of his pants and pulled down his briefs. His cock sprang from beneath his clothing, as hard as steel. Demi greedily clasped her fingers around his shaft, her lips ghosting over the tip, causing him to shiver. They were so soft and her breath hot as it danced through her lips and over his velvety skin.

Demi stuck out her tongue and ran it up the length of him, then slowly guided the head of his cock down her throat. The warmth of her mouth made Vincent groan in ecstasy. She hollowed out her cheeks and sucked him deep, lathering her tongue over a large vein on the underside of his shaft that pulsed in her mouth. His eyes snapped shut as he succumbed to her.

How he missed this.

Missed her.

Missed the feel of her from the inside.

Demi moaned her approval as he throbbed inside her mouth and over her tongue. She quickened her pace and tightened her hold on his base. Vincent gripped her hair and pushed her head, forcing himself farther down her throat. She gagged but kept pushing with an eagerness that compelled him to drive her farther past her limits.

"Good girl," he said, both of his hands in her hair now. "Take it."

Demi looked up at him with teary eyes and fondled his balls with her fingers. Fuck, she was beautiful with her lips wrapped around him, sucking the very soul from his body. Vincent gripped her hair tighter and thrust himself into her harder, a garbled whimper vibrated over his engorged shaft.

"Goddamn it!" he hissed between his clenched teeth, thrusting hard again just to hear her whimper once more. His tip assaulted the back of her throat. He watched a stream of tears fall down her cheeks, her eyes fixed on him, nails biting into his knees as she held on for dear life. He was about to combust, he could feel his climax coming, but it was too quick—*too fucking soon*.

Vincent pulled her off of him, revealing a line of silk from her full lips to him. He pushed his thumb into her mouth, clutching her chin firmly with his fingers. She immediately closed her lips around his thumb, biting softly.

"Stand up and take off my shirt."

She obliged with a grin, rising to her feet before him, pulling at the buttons of the shirt she had borrowed. One by one, tantalizingly slow. Vincent gently stroked himself as he watched her heavy breasts emerge from beneath the fabric. His mouth watered at the sight of them, her dark areolas practically begged to be sucked.

There was something about her wearing his clothes this last week, how they hugged her curves in all the right places.

And the knowledge that she wore nothing beneath them.

No panties, no bra.

He had seen the way her nipples pressed against the fabric of his white shirt the first day after she came out of the shower. Her skin had been so damp that when she put it on, the fabric had become translucent enough for him to see them as clearly as if she had nothing on. He could see the lining of her bare ass, and when she moved just right, the shirt had bared it for him completely. Vincent was instantly thrust back to the first time his hands had cupped those perfect tits and slapped that round ass to the point that it was red and hot to the touch.

The shirt crumpled to the floor around her feet and Demi stood there stark naked, patiently awaiting his next command. He looked up at her, his jaw tense, and ran his tongue over his bottom lip. She was an absolute vision and he planned on devouring every last ounce of her.

"Ride me," he demanded, his voice so deep and bestial that he almost didn't recognize himself.

He needed her. Like a savage beast, he needed to be buried deep inside her.

Demi climbed into his lap and aligned his dick with her entrance, coating his tip in her arousal. Then she slowly sheathed him within her, inch by inch, until she was fully seated on his length. Her mouth opened like she might scream, but no sound escaped—just a sharp intake of breath as he filled her tight pussy to capacity, pushing against her inner walls that deliciously squeezed him back. Demi's hair fell into her face as she looked down at the way he stretched her apart. They both watched, raging lust swirling through the air between them, as she lifted off him only to come back down, his tip hitting that sweet spot inside. She moaned, her hips undulating as she rode him hard and steady.

"Good God, look at you..." Vincent said through clenched teeth. "Look at how good you take me."

A guttural growl rolled in his chest at how wet she was, how her muscles contracted around him, her breasts bouncing before his eyes. He captured one of her nipples between his teeth. She squealed, her sex gushing over him, and quickened her pace. Gripping her hips firmly, digging his fingers into her skin, Vincent moved her faster, lathering his tongue over the sensitive bud.

"Vin-Vincent!" Demi screamed. She came hard, her pussy dripping wet, clenching him so fucking tight. She slumped into his chest, his cock still filling her, painfully erect.

Grabbing her by the jaw, he forced her to look up at him, then crashed his lips against hers in a bruising kiss. Pushing his tongue into her mouth, he swept it over hers, eliciting a lustrous moan from her throat. Her hips worked against his so sweetly, his cock throbbing in response. Pulling away with her jaw still in his grasp, he snarled, "I hope you don't think I'm anywhere near done with that pussy, Dem."

She smiled, a wicked look in her eyes. "I'd be thoroughly disappointed if you were, Officer Kore."

Vincent's hand slid from her jaw down to her throat. The other hand held her as he stood with her legs wrapped tightly around him. Squeezing her throat, he kissed her again. Demi's fingers wound through his hair and tugged gently.

The feel of her lips on his, the smell of her sweet breath—it had been all he could think about, *dream* about, during their time apart. Finally, he had her again, with no restrictions, no danger of someone catching them in an unspeakable act. They were free to fuck as loud and ruthless as they desired.

Her tongue danced with his, her fingers now clawing at his ample shoulders. Vincent relished the pain from her nails digging and cutting into him, his cock twitching inside her.

He walked them up to the back of the couch and then released her. Demi's feet hit the ground and she stood before him. Looking down, he saw his dick glistening wet from being within the confines of her delectable cunt.

"Turn around," he instructed so she did. Grabbing her waist from behind, Vincent forced her to bend over and then hiked up one of her legs. Her knee was now resting on the back of the couch and her face was pushed into the cushions. Her pussy gleamed up at him, dripping wet and rosy from being impaled on his girth moments before.

Stroking himself with one hand, he tenderly ran his middle finger through her glistening folds, gingerly dipping it into her slit. Demi's hips rolled and she whimpered in response as he proceeded to fondle her clit. Then, without warning, he drove himself deep into her. She cried out so loud that her voice rebounded off the walls surrounding them. The sting assaulted his ears as he began fucking her relentlessly from behind. Demi shrieked again, clutching at the cushions of the couch beneath her.

"One more," he demanded, his voice deep and ferocious. He plunged harder, slapping her ass. Demi screamed. "*Come on*, give me one more!"

He slapped her again and again until her ass was a vibrant red through the toasted golden hue of her skin. She screamed with the rolling wave of her orgasm crashing down over her again.

"Fuck, I love it when you come for me," Vincent growled. "Don't *ever* keep this pussy from me again. Do you hear me?"

"Yes!" she screamed, her voice muffled in the cushion and her body shaking beneath his grasp.

The sight of her ass pounding against him, his balls slapping her clit over and over, was driving him mad with desire.

He had to have more of her.

Without losing his rhythm, Vincent lifted her other leg onto the back of the couch, suspending her off the ground. Then he grabbed her throat from behind with both hands, forcing her to arch her back in what had to be a painful position.

But he didn't care because he knew the little siren loved it.

She felt so tight in this state that he began to see stars. Squeezing her throat tighter and pounding even faster, Vincent erupted and came deep inside her, yelling her name. His seed spilled into her, mixing with her own arousal, seeping out of her and down his thighs.

W-wait—his mind was fuzzy, eyelids heavy—*what did I just call her?*

He slumped over. Her hair tickled his nose and he breathed heavily, trying to think straight. He realized he had not called her Demi.

Fuck, I said "Prue."

Vincent sat up and immediately began to apologize, but when Demi turned to face him, she kissed him, trapping his apology inside. The worry eddied from his mind and a lascivious fog settled around them as he relished their kiss.

Fuck, this feels good. She feels so *good.*

Chapter 9

It was like living the perspective of the box just after Pandora opened it, subjecting the world to what simmered inside. No one ever thought about the box itself, the wear and tear it must have endured holding those emotions within it for so long. It could be inferred that the box did not mind these terrors escaping, no matter what effect they were sure to have on the world. Anger, fear, hopelessness, and madness fled from inside Prudence and left her feeling weightless. It left her feeling so full of hope.

Thanks to Vincent.

In her session with Osiris the evening before, they had delved deep into her connection with Vincent, which brought her both clarity and dread. There was no denying how much he meant to her and how compatible they had come to be. However, her affliction would always pose a problem—this nasty dark side of her that drove her to do unspeakable things.

Things she wasn't so sure she regretted.

Things, at times, she enjoyed.

Prudence peered over at Vincent as he drove them to the storage lot where Ms. Rizzo held all of Prudence's belongings. For the first time in weeks, she didn't sense an inkling of desire compounded by dread and rage, though she was not left with that too-familiar numbness she usually strived to obtain. Instead, she felt warm, light, at ease—feelings so good, she wished in that moment, gazing at Vincent, that she would never feel numb again.

Was he the cure?

The antidote to her affliction?

"Dem," Vincent said, his eyes on the road, freeing her from her loving trance. "I have to apologize."

She blinked. "For?"

He rubbed his chin thoughtfully, ruffling his beard, and said, "For uh... calling you Prue. I lost it for a minute at the end and wasn't thinking."

Prudence smiled. She didn't mind in the slightest, though she appreciated his dedication to her healing and becoming this *Demi*.

In her heart, she wasn't quite there yet. She *was* still Prue.

"No apologies are necessary. It was an honest mistake," she reassured him, running her fingers through his beard to fix it for him. Vincent stilled beneath her touch, clearly unaccustomed to her displaying affection of any kind.

That will change, she thought.

They rolled to a stop light and Vincent released the steering wheel, scratching the back of his neck. Prudence watched as his face blushed into a bright pink. "I should also apologize for, you know, coming in you. But don't worry. We can stop and get a Plan B on our way home."

His crystal eyes gleamed in the light, a translucent pair of portals to his benevolent soul. Prudence knew he wasn't by any means oblivious to the kind of life she'd lived growing up, but she felt panicked about having to reveal what she was going to say next.

"We don't have to worry about that," she said, sitting up straighter and looking ahead as traffic resumed.

"I think we should. It only takes one..." He trailed off, oddly nervous. They had just fucked like a pair of heathens. How could he feel embarrassed about speaking openly about something as small and insignificant as a single sperm cell?

"Due to my years of abuse, I physically can't conceive children, Vincent. So, no, it wouldn't take one sperm—or even a million, for that matter." She anticipated his grimace, shame blossoming over the palette of her cheeks. She knew it wasn't her fault. Knew that what those men had done to her, what *they* allowed them to do, to cause her uterus to rupture wasn't something she could have stopped. The memory of being in the hospital after the accident and having the doctors inform her, at fourteen years old, that due to the severity of her injury and having gone untreated a hysterectomy was imminent in order to save her life assaulted her mind and dried her throat. Every time was excruciating, there was no telling when it happened.

Get it together, Prue. Shame does not suit you.

"I'm sorry," Vincent said, then rested his hand on her own. He curled his calloused fingers around hers and squeezed gently. She watched the motion, then ran her thumb over his hand. Her digit fell into each divot of his knuckles as she committed this pure sensation to memory.

To remember the feelings that were worth having.

"I've never desired children for fear they'd enter a world like the one I knew. It has always seemed to me that this outcome was for the best," she said.

"I doubt you would have allowed that for your kids if you ever had them," Vincent replied, pulling her hand to his lips. "We're here."

They pulled into the parking lot of a small storage facility. Prudence immediately recognized Ms. Rizzo's box-dyed red hair as the woman emerged from her compact car by the entrance to the lot's office. Ms. Rizzo glanced at Prudence through the window, then looked down at her feet.

This would be uncomfortable.

Even as her superior, Carmina Rizzo hadn't paid much attention to Prudence the few years they had worked together at the firm. Sharp and stoic, Ms. Rizzo had an air about her that could slice through stone like a scalding knife through butter. A powerful, self-made woman who surely worked far harder than her male counterparts, she was someone who demanded—and certainly deserved—respect. Prudence could only imagine what the woman thought of her now after all that had happened.

She and Vincent exited the vehicle, donning their face masks, and Vincent gave Ms. Rizzo a nod in greeting. "Good afternoon, Carmina. It's nice to finally meet you."

In typical Ms. Rizzo fashion, she offered him a cold, even glare before gesturing toward the office and walking inside. Vincent cleared his throat, offered Prudence his arm and they followed her inside. The three of them stood quietly at the front desk, Ms. Rizzo a decent six feet away, if not more, as they waited to be assisted. Of course, she was following CDC guidelines for being out in public during the continued rise of COVID, but Prudence suspected that even if this weren't the case, Ms. Rizzo would keep her distance. Prudence held onto Vincent's arm tighter as she peeked over at Ms. Rizzo.

It was a peculiar feeling Prudence was experiencing. She had never been afraid of the woman in the slightest, but in this moment, the chill coming off her made Prudence shiver.

Intimidation? No. Compounded guilt perhaps?

An attendant came from the door toward the back marked "restroom" and greeted them. Ms. Rizzo gave him the key for the storage unit and her information, "I've already paid for the month. However, if Mr. Kore intends to utilize the unit past the end of the month, I'd like to have it changed over into his name."

Vincent agreed and the attendant started working on the transition. Once everything was changed over, Vincent retrieved the keys and they walked out, Ms. Rizzo getting a head start.

She was quick in getting to her car, like she was running from an encroaching wave sure to wreak havoc and bring anguish and despair. Prudence's heart began to pound. Despite her nerves, she worried that she wouldn't get a chance to speak with her.

"Carmina, wait!" Prudence called out, unlocking her arm from Vincent's. It was an act she immediately regretted as she stood there by herself. She felt as if she were alone in a raft in the middle of the ocean and now Carmina Rizzo was the wave.

Ms. Rizzo froze, her manicured hand wrapped around the car door handle. Then, with as much indifference as she could muster, she turned to face Prudence and waited for her to continue. Nerves swelled in Prudence's belly, causing the butterflies to go berserk.

Fuck.

Folding her arms around her stomach to soothe it, Prudence took a step closer and said, "Thank you for handling my affairs while I was away."

"You mean in jail?" Ms. Rizzo bit back, her first words to Prudence thoroughly disarming.

Prudence visibly wilted like a dying flower.

Seemingly unfazed by Prudence's shift in demeanor, Ms. Rizzo continued. "Had I not already been aware of your lack of a family, I would have rejected the responsibility. You're lucky that after the news released the deplorable story of your transgressions, I didn't have all of your belongings trashed. Mrs. Hale had been a prominent figure in this community for decades before you murdered her of your own unfounded volition. After today, I want nothing more to do with the likes of *you*."

Tears welled up in Prudence's eyes, distorting her vision as she listened, knowing undoubtedly that she deserved every agonizing word—and more.

"I'm so sorry," Prudence replied, surprised at how her voice shook. She could feel Vincent approach from behind. His hands rested on her shoulders as a tear broke free. "You won't hear from me ever again, I assure you."

Without another word, Ms. Rizzo got into her car and drove away.

Vincent wrapped his arms around Prudence and held her close as more tears escaped down her cheeks.

◆

Once they got home, Vincent helped Demi wash all her clothes. Almost a year in a climate-controlled unit had left her belongings smelling stale. From the storage unit, they took only her clothes, her shoes, and a few small things, leaving all her furniture and kitchenware behind. Perhaps they'd have a better idea of what to do with everything by the time the month was over.

Now, seated on his bed, Vincent watched Demi as she pristinely folded her warm, clean clothes, which he handed to her from a basket on the floor beside the bed. She seemed to have calmed down substantially since they'd returned to the apartment, now meticulously concentrating on a chore she had clearly missed during her incarceration.

"I bet you're excited to finally wear your own clothes again," he said, a smirk lifting one corner of his mouth.

"I'd walk around naked at all times if the weather and society permitted it," Demi replied. She peeked up at him and gave him a charming wink.

Vincent laughed. "I don't know about you, but I've never cared much for what society thinks."

Her irises glittered before she looked back down at the skirt she was folding. God, he was enjoying this. She was finally loosening up and even being playful in a way he had not yet seen.

He hoped for more of it.

"How would you feel about meeting my mom?" Vincent asked, handing her another shirt.

Demi took it. "I would like that very much. I haven't had a chance to thank her yet for the gift."

"She's invited us over for dinner next week so she can finally meet you."

"You mean so she can determine for herself that I won't murder you?" Demi asked.

His eyes shot over to her in shock. She smiled wide.

"That was dark!" he replied, a nervous laugh released the tension in his chest.

"Sorry, it was funnier in my head," she said with a passive shrug.

Once they had finished the basket, Vincent showed her where he had made room in his drawers and closet for her clothes. They fell into a rhythm putting everything away. Then Prudence asked, "How did your father pass?"

Fuck if she didn't know how to say *exactly* the right thing to throw him off guard.

Vincent paused and rubbed the back of his neck. "He had leukemia."

"Were you young when it happened?" she continued.

"Not really. I was in my early twenties at the time." He closed the drawer that he had neatly arranged her workout gear into. "Why do you ask?"

Demi sat on the bed, looking up at him. Her eyes were large and full of wonder, though laced with sadness. She said, "When you told me he had died, I realized just how little I actually know about you. This whole time, it's all been about me and my past. We've never discussed you and yours." She reached up and took his hand in hers.

"I want to know everything. When is your birthday? Where did you go to school? What are your parents' names? Who was your first love and your first heartbreak? What makes you happy? What makes you sad?"

"Wow, um..." Vincent was stumped. He sat beside her, still holding her hand, and decided to start with her first question. "I was born November 8, 1989. I went to Husson University, which is where I met Joe."

"You've known each other a long time," Demi said.

"Yeah, he's the big brother I never had. When Dad died, he was there for me through the whole thing. I don't think I would have graduated if it weren't for him keeping my ass in line," Vincent recalled.

"You're fortunate to have him."

He nodded in response with a smile, then wondered if she had ever had a good friend in her life.

"My dad's name was Stephanos Kore and my mom is Nerina. They were both born in Greece. My mom lived there until she was twelve or thirteen. Dad came to the States when he was four."

"Did they ever take you to Greece?" Demi asked.

"Sure, many times. We spent summers overseas while I was growing up. It was like my second home." His tone grew somber. "We haven't been back since Dad died though and our plans have been delayed thanks to the pandemic. Mom was crushed when we had to cancel our flight."

Demi laid on her side, propping her head up with her hand, and Vincent followed suit. She was charming in her curiosity as she continued asking him questions about his family in Greece. He told her about his Yia Yia, who couldn't have been taller than five feet, with hands as soft and fragile as tissue paper. He told her about the parties they had, the trips to Myrtos beach where they would swim down into the underwater caves and collect the roundest pebbles they could find along the coastal line. He told her about riding bikes with his favorite cousins, Niko and Artimus, eating droves of loukoumades that left its sticky nectar all over their faces and hands.

Then came the time for her next question: his first love and first heartbreak. They were one and the same.

"Her name was Calista Miron. We grew up together. Our families are pretty close thanks to our being the only Greeks in our neighborhood. She was my first crush, first girlfriend, first everything." Vincent trailed off, his gaze distant.

"What happened?" Demi asked.

He redirected his attention to her. She was now lying on her stomach, her curls cascading over her shoulder. One lock covered her face, and he reached up and tucked it behind her ear. "We were together for several years," he said. "Then, when we were twenty, she realized I wasn't what she wanted. Looking back on it, I see why, but at the time it felt like my world was falling apart. I was alone for a long time after that. I've had a few girlfriends since but nothing substantial."

"Why weren't you what she wanted?"

It was like Demi was twisting the dagger lodged in his heart with her direct questions about something he had long since buried. Not that he still longed for Calista. She was married now with three kids and lived states away with her little family. He "liked" her family photos on social media and wished her well from the depths of his heart, but he knew for certain that he wasn't the one for her and she wasn't the one for him.

"We disagreed on a fundamental level about certain things. When we were kids, it was easy. Life was easy. She liked ice cream, so did I. I liked playing board games, so did she. But as we grew older, the less we saw eye to eye on the real things that mattered. Our views didn't align."

Demi looked away from him for the first time in what felt like hours. She hid her eyes when she asked, "Do you still miss her?"

"No. Not anymore," he replied with certitude. She seemed to like his answer when she rolled back over to face him.

Demi reached out to him, running her finger up and down the length of his forearm. "What makes you happy?"

"Huh... what makes me happy." Vincent scratched his chin as he racked his brain for an honest response. "Well, a number of things, I guess."

"Like what? Name five things."

He smiled. "Uh, my ivy plants out there on the shelf. I propagated them myself."

Her eyes widened. "Did you really?"

"Yup, I did. Took a few trimmings from my mom's ivy."

Demi smiled wide. "That's impressive, Vincent."

"Nah, I'm alright. Number two, Brocc makes me happy. He's a mess, but I love him. So does my friendship with Joe, so that makes three. And good food!"

She laughed, scooting closer into him. "Ok, that's four. And the last one?"

Vincent breathed in her scent, her body so close now. "You."

"Me?" She flinched. "How so?"

"Helping you, spending time with you, watching you get better day by day. Being with you. It all makes me happy." Vincent studied her for a moment as she took in his every word. He reached for her, wrapping his arm around her waist, and pulled her flush against him, leaving not a centimeter of space between them.

She did not resist.

Instead, Demi nuzzled up against him, her face buried in his chest. "Nothing makes me happier than when I'm with you, Vincent."

He stroked her back tenderly. She didn't ask her last question: What made him sad. But he wanted her to know that too.

"The hardships you suffered make me sad. Thinking about how you were hurt by the people you were supposed to trust most in this world makes me sad. And angry, if I'm honest."

Demi pulled away from him slightly to look up into his face. "You don't need to feel sad for me."

"But I do."

"Tell me what else makes you sad," Demi said, looping her legs securely through his. " I want to know so that I can protect you the way you protect me."

Vincent's heart clenched hard in his chest. She was opening up so much more now than ever before, both physically and emotionally. He was astounded by her.

“Thinking about my dad in his last days,” he replied. “I love talking about him and reminiscing on the good times. Just not those last few days in the hospital. The thought of him like that hurts too much.”

She nodded, “Understood.”

“Number four—we’re still going up to five things, right?”

Demi laughed. “Of course, why not?”

“Number four, seeing my mom cry. As unflinching and stoic as she is, crying is rare, but when her tears start to flow, it’s like a bullet to the chest. And number five is season two, episode nine of ‘Louie.’”

“I’ve never seen it,” Demi said. “I don’t watch television.”

“I’ll have to show it to you some time. Louis C.K. is controversial now, but his show was pure gold,” he said. “Well, the episode is pretty sad and fucked up. Makes you really think about how we live our lives and what we leave behind, if anything at all.”

“Like a legacy.”

“Exactly. Sometimes I wonder if I’ll leave anything of worth behind when I go. If I’m even worthy of being remembered.”

“Why would you think you're unworthy of being remembered?” she asked.

"I don't know," Vincent shrugged. "Part of me is ashamed of the mistakes I've made, the choices I made in taking advantage of you the way that I did, whether you see it that way or not. I try to be the man my father was, but feel like I'm always falling short. Maybe since he passed I've created this grandiose inflated image of what he was in my mind and I'm aiming way too high."

Demi took his hand into hers and said, "You're worthy to me, Vincent Kore, and I know without a doubt Stephanos would be proud of the man you have become."

The wind fled his body as if a wildfire had broken out and consumed every ounce of oxygen surrounding them. Vincent couldn't think of what to say or how to express what her words had meant to him. So he leaned in, placed a kiss to her forehead and peeled himself away from her to stand. "It's getting late. I have to walk Brocc before bed." Then he was out the door.

◆

It was all so much, so quickly.

Like a seal had been broken, allowing Demi to finally be free to express her feelings, and all of those hidden pieces of her were bobbing to the surface. They were pieces he was glad yet overwhelmed to experience. The way she moved into him, the adoration in her expression when she looked at him. The playful way she spoke. He felt honored but worried that if she perceived any apprehension from his bewilderment by all that was happening, she would shrivel up and scurry away. He didn't want to discourage her, so before that could happen, he left for a little air.

Brocc trotted eagerly down the road, nose to the ground in search of his regular spots to pee. Vincent had put Brocc in his little coat and booties to keep warm against the plummeting temperatures of the night. The weather was predicted to get down to twenty-eight degrees.

A perfect night to share a bed with Demi.

Vincent shook the thought from his head. Too much, too soon could be counterproductive. Besides he had a fine heater to keep him warm.

This wouldn't be his first cold night alone.

Though he'd be a liar if he said he didn't long for someone next to him—especially someone so dear to him.

Brocc finished his business and started back home, with Vincent dragging a little behind.

CHAPTER 10

Prudence lay awake, staring into the depthless black ceiling above her. She couldn't sleep. When Vincent and Broccoli had returned to the apartment, Vincent had taken a shower, wished her a good night with a gentle kiss, and then left her alone in his bed. She tossed and turned, surrounded by the essence of him trapped in the bedding, vanilla musk stimulating her senses, but it wasn't enough.

It wasn't him.

Was she going out of her mind? Was she obsessed?

Was she in—*No, go to sleep!*

But she couldn't. She just fucking couldn't rest with Vincent so close yet so far. She tried humming "Dear, Prudence" in the hopes that it would help like it always did in calming her down, but it made no difference. The song that her so-called father had called hers no longer comforted her like it used to.

Maybe some hot chamomile with honey would help, she thought, *but what if he doesn't have chamomile?*

Then hot water would have to do.

Prudence tossed the covers aside, wrapped herself in her warm, freshly clean robe, and exited the room. She quietly made her way into the kitchen, sparing a passing glance at Vincent's motionless form on the couch. He was lying on his back, one arm folded behind his head, the other on his broad chest.

Prudence searched the cabinets for tea, but she couldn't focus on what was in front of her.

Too distracted by what was behind her.

Fuck the tea.

After shutting the cabinet, she folded her arms tightly over the robe and slowly walked over to Vincent. Broccoli, on the rug beside the couch, whimpered softly as she approached. His nub of a tail wagged excitedly. Prudence looked at him with a small smile and lifted a finger to her lips. Broccoli harrumphed and lowered his head, his tail never ceasing.

She knelt beside the couch. Vincent did not stir. His chest continued to rise and fall with his steady breaths. She almost didn't want to wake him as she watched him lying there so serenely. Gently, Prudence caressed his face and cooed his name.

Nothing.

"Vincent?" she said again.

He inhaled sharply, wriggling awake. His eyes cracked open to the sight of her. For a second she worried he'd be upset, but the worry was washed away with the immediate concern in his eyes.

"Dem? Are you ok?" he asked, now looking around the room, presumably for anything amiss.

Prudence took his hand. Warmth bloomed behind her rib cage at the feel of his skin over hers.

"I'm fine," she said.

Vincent watched her now, stroking her hair and neck as if to settle her, reassurance in his touch. She leaned into his hand, her eyelashes fluttering, as she melted for him. "I can't sleep. Would you join me in the room?"

His thumb trailed over her throat, then back to the side of her neck.

Prudence trembled.

"Sure, if that will help," Vincent replied, his voice like dusty gravel.

Prudence nodded and rose slowly from her knees. Her robe fell open, revealing pert nipples through her camisole and a pair of black lace panties. Vincent's throat bobbed, his eyes scouring her quickly before standing. They descended into the bedroom, with Vincent closing the door behind them to keep Broccoli out.

She was removing her robe to get back into bed when a stream of moonlight seeped in and bathed her in its soft, effervescent glow. When she turned to the window, there stood Vincent. He had pulled the black-out curtain to the side and tucked it away letting in the pale light. He stared, a desperate, unmistakable longing in his gaze.

He cleared his throat. "I'm sorry, I don't know what I was thinking. I'll close them—"

Prudence shook her head, stopping him.

He wanted to see her and she wanted to be seen.

Slowly, she pulled her camisole up and over her head, letting it fall to the floor beside the robe. Vincent's eyes were fixed on her as she trailed her hands over the knoll of her breasts, then down her tummy, sliding her fingers beneath the band of her panties. Within seconds, they, too, were on the floor.

Vincent came up to her, his breath warm against her neck as he placed a kiss on her skin. Prudence stood achingly still, reveling in the sensation of his hands running up the sides of her waist.

She wanted his hands everywhere all at once.

They were warm and firm as they kneaded her sweltering flesh. His lips finally found hers and he kissed her with abandon.

Vincent walked her back into the bed and held her to him as he lowered them both onto the mattress. He tasted divine, Prudence thought, as their tongues intertwined. The weight of him over her, the press of his hardened cock through his sweatpants against her inner thigh—it was all so exhilarating. She wiggled beneath him, her sex pulsing, and opened her legs wider.

Vincent thrust his pelvis against her, grinding into her bare, already soaking-wet pussy. Prudence moaned, her body shuddering beneath him.

"Do you want me to fuck you, Demi?" Vincent whispered in her ear.

"Yes," she replied instantly.

"Or..." He thrust against her again, sensuous and slow. "Do you want me to make love to you?"

Prudence heard him but didn't at the same time.

Make love?

He wanted to make love to her? What would that entail?

Did she want whatever lovemaking was, or did she want to be fucked hard and mercilessly? Now, given the option, she wasn't sure.

She had never experienced anything but the latter except… except for the second time they'd been together. In the shower of solitary after she'd opened her soul up to him.

That hadn't felt like any of her other sexual encounters.

At that moment, she had felt more connected to him than anyone before, more connected to herself and in tune with her own body. It had felt like all the wrongs in the world had been made right, like for the first time she was exactly where she needed to be. There hadn't been and could never be someone other than him after that.

Was that feeling akin to love?

Vincent looked her in the eyes, continuing to grind into her, ready for anything, yet hoping for something in particular. As her eyelids grew heavier and her breaths came in faster, she began to think that maybe she wanted that particular something too.

"Love," she said, her voice shaking. "Make love to me."

Without another word, Vincent kissed her again, his lips delicately capturing and releasing hers. There was no doubt in her mind that her life could be sustained by his kisses alone. She hungered for little else. As he satiated her appetite for his lips, Vincent ran his fingers through the petals between her legs. He dipped one thick finger into her, like a wick through hot wax. Her hips undulated in response, her hands clasping to the hard muscles of his arms. With his finger, coated in her arousal, he circled her clit, sending shockwaves through her system. Prudence let out a moan. His lips parted from hers to set it free. Again, his finger pushed through her folds, wetter than they had been moments before, then continued his torturous circles.

"Mmm, you're always so ready for me." His lips found her nipple and teased the firm bud with his tongue as he gently sucked.

She took in a sharp breath, her focus resting solely on the building pleasure within her center, and whispered a grateful, "Yes."

"I know, Demi. I know." Dipping two fingers within her this time, Vincent quickened the pace at which he fondled her clit, nipping at her breast. He carried on like this for what felt like forever, or perhaps it had been mere seconds. Prudence had no concept of time in the seconds or minutes or hours he spent pleasuring her. All she could fathom in this instant was the electricity pulsing through her, from the bottoms of her feet to the tips of her ears. Before she knew it, every nerve in her body was stimulated all at once and her climax took over, exploding from the depths of her soul.

She cried out, her voice carrying on the wave of her orgasm, the nectar of her arousal soaking the sheets beneath her. Vincent lathered his tongue once again over her nipple as the last dregs of her climax extinguished and she was returned to reality.

Her brain was mush, her body limp, as she focused on her labored breathing. She didn't even notice Vincent remove those sinful sweatpants until his bare knees nudged against her inner thighs to open them. Prudence looked up at him and, without a thought, she cupped his face in her hands, ran her thumbs over the stubble of his jaw, and pulled him down for a kiss. He took his cock and slowly led it to her entrance, running the head through her drenched petals.

Teasing her even more.

He drove his tongue into her mouth. Prudence captured it between her lips and sucked. Lifting her hips off the bed, she pressed herself against him, pleading with him to penetrate her. Vincent groaned against her mouth and sheathed himself within her. His girth stretched and filled her so completely, she couldn't hold back her cries, tightening around his cock.

"Fuck, Demi," he hissed through gritted teeth, eyes ablaze as he did his best to maintain a slow, even pace. "You feel so fucking good, I could come right now."

He retreated slowly, inch by exquisite inch, until he was out and crawled from on top of her. "But I won't."

Prudence's mind scattered as she frantically reached for him to come back, to finish her off. Before she could cry out in protest, he buried his face between her thighs, his tongue plunging within her pussy.

She gasped, falling back into the mattress and arching her back. Vincent devoured her, licking and sucking like she were the ripest, juiciest fruit he could find in an oasis surrounded by desert. Deeper and deeper his tongue slithered until she came unraveled once again. Prudence dug at his shoulders, pulling and tugging at him. "Please, Vincent. I need you inside me, *please*."

Vincent lunged forward at her command and mounted her again. He plunged within her to the hilt, Prudence's legs wrapped around his waist, opening herself wide for him. She wanted him as deep as he could go, even if it tore her in half.

"Yes," she whispered as he quickened his pace.

Vincent took her legs one at a time and rested them on either of his shoulders.

"Yes."

He pushed them farther into her, sinking his cock deeper.

"Yes," she said louder.

Prudence could feel her knees press into her chest as he bent her in half and thrust harder.

"Yes!" she screamed.

She couldn't get enough of him in this position, felt completely enthralled in him and connected like before. They were one, fused by desire, hunger, devotion. Nails digging into his forearms, Prudence came again, her legs shaking, her skin tingling. She could feel her arousal dripping down between their fervent skin.

Vincent hissed at the feel of her pulsating cunt. "That's it, Demi, take what you need."

Prudence was being driven over the edge. It was all so consuming. She looked up at him with pleading eyes, her lips in a full, luscious pout.

"You're so beautiful," he said, his eyelids heavy.

He was close.

"Come for me, Vincent," she demanded. "I want to feel you burst inside me."

His eyes rolled back in his head, his face etched with elation as his climax found him. He did as she asked and came deep within the chasm of her sex. A warmth filled her core, and the moment he pulled out of her, he unfolded her body and held her close. With his hands, Vincent kneaded and rubbed her lower back and hips, anticipating the dull ache that slowly started to set in now that the heat surrounding them dissipated.

She adored this man so much that well over a year ago she would have deemed it impossible. Impossible not because she lacked the emotional capacity to care for someone else but because she simply could not bring herself to do so. Never meeting a soul worthy of her affection and time, she would not allow it. But now, wrapped in his arms, settled in the only place on Earth she longed to be, there was no doubting what was blossoming within her previously calloused heart. Still, a persistent fear kept the bloom stifled and at bay.

A pain settled within her chest. *What am I going to do?*

CHAPTER 11

February 1999

T*he audacity of that fucking brat to bang on our door at 7:00 am like she was* actually *going to school after that bullshit she pulled with the school counselor.*

Lara could barely see straight as she made pancakes for them after Sam's insistence that they apologize.

She's just a kid, he said, *this is going to be a big change for her. I think you should apologize, doll.*

Apologize for what? Prue *is the one who almost got us investigated by fucking CPS!* Lara thought.

Well, she and that pig that Sam had lent the girl out to.

Why did he have to be so rough with her and leave marks? she wondered, scowling as she washed the mixing bowl from their "family" breakfast that morning. If Prue had just worn the long-sleeved shirt Lara had told her to wear, that nosey teacher of hers wouldn't have noticed the bruises and wouldn't have brought it up to the counselor in the first place. She took a long drag of the cigarette that hung from her lips as she stood at the sink.

Stupid little girl.

Sam had never left marks like that on her at the beginning of their relationship. Maybe she was just lucky.

No, not maybe. I'm very lucky to have Sam.

Sam had been a coworker of her father's when they met. It was "bring your kid to work day" at the office and even though eleven-year-old Lara had no interest in learning about her father's day-to-day life in HR, she was glad to have gone when she laid her eyes on Sam. He worked in the sales department and had been in the common room enjoying a cup of coffee when she wandered in to get a snack. Her father had given her a couple of dollars for the vending machine.

"Whose daughter might you be?" Sam asked, winking at her as he took a sip from his paper coffee cup. He was lean, with dark brown hair and the prettiest hazel eyes with flecks of gold she had ever seen.

Lara blushed deeply, her tummy squirming like she had swallowed a pound of eels. "Bill Parkin's."

"Good guy, Bill. What are you, fifteen? Sixteen?" he asked. He looked like Dallas Winston from The Outsiders the way he leaned nonchalantly against the counter beside the vending machine.

Lara giggled profusely at his assumption that she was so old. "No, I'm eleven!"

The corner of his mouth lifted and nervously he ran his fingers through his hair. "Wow, forgive me. You just look so... mature."

He finished his coffee and said he had to go but asked if she had an email so they could continue their conversation later. Lara eagerly gave it to him and, over the course of a few weeks, he romanced her through their emails. She talked to him like she had never dreamed of speaking to anyone before, let alone a man twelve years her senior.

A man who thought she was mature and beautiful for her age.

She was over the moon about him, and when he finally asked to meet up for their first date, she did not hesitate to accept. Lara asked her mom to drive her to the mall to meet up with friends. Once she was dropped off and her mother had driven out of sight, Sam pulled up in his car. He took her back to his apartment, where he had prepared dinner and drinks. Lara had never tried alcohol before, but he assured her she wouldn't even taste it once he mixed it with Coke. It was only partially true, but she enjoyed it all the same. Their romantic dinner turned into cuddling on the couch with a movie. Before she knew it, it was 7:30 at night.

"Shit!" she exclaimed, looking at her watch. "Mom will be at the mall to pick me up any minute!"

Sam wrapped his arms around her, pulling her to him, "Oh, but you can't leave yet." He kissed her neck.

Lara froze.

"Um. I really should go." Nerves welled up inside her as his kisses progressed, his hold tightening.

"*Not* until the date is over," he said firmly. Sam took her hand and shoved it between his legs. She could feel the firm swell of his manhood through his jeans.

She was petrified.

"You wouldn't want to leave me like this, would you?" Sam asked, grinding into her hand.

Lara had no idea what he meant. She wasn't altogether certain what was happening between his legs, let alone what she was supposed to do about it. She guessed that perhaps he wanted her to kiss him back. A knot formed in her belly. "Well... no?"

She kissed him quickly on the lips, hoping that would help, but he just smiled wide and pulled her in for another. This time, he stuck his tongue in her mouth. When she tried to pull away, his grip on her tightened painfully.

"Have you ever had sex?" he asked, his hands roaming in places she'd never been touched. She felt icky inside.

"No," she replied, trying to remain as still as possible, afraid to admit that she had never heard of it.

"I can teach you," Sam offered, laying her down on the couch, not waiting for her reply. What happened next was far more painful than she had imagined anything could be, but he was gentle. And the numerous times after that grew less and less painful until she was really starting to enjoy herself.

God, I'm so lucky.

Prudence sat in the living room now, humming her song as she colored in her Strawberry Shortcake coloring book. Lara frowned at the back of the child's head, hating her and hating that grating song. Every time Sam played it to cheer the girl up, it made Lara regret more and more having chosen that damn name. How was she supposed to know it was also the name of one of The Beatles' most popular songs?

Fuck Prudence and fuck The Beatles too.

The only thing the girl was good for was the cash she generated from the clients Sam lent her out to. It was so much money that Lara didn't have to work anymore. When they got Prue as a baby, Lara had to get a job to help support their "family."

After she ran away with Sam at twelve, he had to quit his job and start up somewhere new. The new job paid enough to get them both by, but with a baby, he couldn't do it on his own.

She resented Prue for that too.

Now, with the cash flow coming in, she understood what all the trouble was for. Even if she had to continue playing house, and share Sam with the little shit, the money was well worth it.

For now, at least.

Most of all, she resented how much Sam adored the girl. He showed her more attention as the years passed, making Lara jealous beyond belief. He let Prue get away with everything, never spanking her or showing her his rage like he had Lara. He really and truly treated her like he was her father. As if he wasn't selling her to grown men for sex. As if he wasn't the mastermind behind it all.

And though she couldn't admit it to herself yet, the way he looked at Prue was starting to change. The way he stood outside her door and listened in when a John was in her room.

Lara shook her head of the thought, loaded up the drying rack, and snuffed out her cigarette in an ashtray on the counter. She then told Prue to stay put while she went to shower. Sam had left for work about an hour ago and she knew leaving the girl alone for even twenty minutes could result in disaster. "If you touch anything other than those crayons I'll whip you."

Prue nodded, tears lining her eyes. Lara hated how the girl used her tears to manipulate.

You don't fool me, you little bitch.

Before she could head down the hall toward her bedroom, a knock sounded on the door. A knot formed in her stomach. They weren't expecting company, so, naturally, her mind went to the worst possible scenarios: CPS or the police.

"Don't move," Lara ordered Prue as she made her way to the door. When she looked through the peephole, her apprehension faded and was quickly replaced by annoyance. She swung the door open to find Ramona and that fucking kid she had called about last week.

"What the fuck are you doing here?" Lara growled, crossing her arms over her chest.

"Hello to you too, Lara," Ramona replied, "Can we come in?"

"No. What you can do is turn your ass around and get off my property, and take that snot-nose brat with you. I told you we didn't want him." Lara looked down at the boy, who stood shyly at Ramona's feet, and grimaced.

She said his name was Dante. He was two.

"Listen, you've had success with Prue, right?" Ramona asked. "Imagine if you had a girl *and* a boy to turn out. Think of the money you could make with Dante!"

"Then why don't *you* do it? The girl is enough. Too much to tell the truth, so why don't you just fuck off!" Lara screamed.

Ramona did not flinch, but the moment her eyes drifted past Lara, she recoiled. Confused, Lara turned around to find Prue standing there, staring at Ramona.

Lara slapped Prue across the face hard enough to sting her own hand. "Didn't I tell you not to move?"

Prue started to cry and retreated to the couch, holding onto her cheek.

Turning back to Ramona, Lara said, "The answer is no. Don't call and don't show up here ever again. Next time you do, I'll make sure you regret it."

Lara slammed the door in Ramona and Dante's faces and went into the living room to deal with Prue and her defiance.

She'll learn to listen.

Chapter 12

May 2020

Broccoli joined Vincent and Prudence that morning on their run. Vincent had been right about the dog's stubby legs not allowing him to keep up. They had to cut the run short after a mile because the pup refused to continue past Center and Congress.

Once they got home, they shared a pot of coffee over a breakfast of yogurt and granola. Prudence found the food to be unbelievably satisfying. In fact, she got a second serving—something completely unheard of for her. Typically, she struggled with each bite, but today, after their run, numerous laughs with Broccoli, and now being seated across from Vincent with their feet winding around each other under the table, Prudence couldn't get enough of it all. When Gerty visited that afternoon, she felt a fullness in her heart that left her entire body stained in a warm blush.

Gerty stayed for a few hours and vented about the state of everything at the prison. She said inmates were still coming forward with their accounts of what Benetiz had done to them. Gerty grimaced every time she uttered his name. Prudence knew it was only a matter of time before Warden Seifert called her in to give her account of events to the court. Two of the various stipulations of her release included keeping quiet about what actually happened and testifying on behalf of the prison.

It was easy enough to be evasive about the truth, but outright lying would be a struggle for her. As she had once told Vincent those many months ago in solitary, she was not *keen* on lying.

Perhaps it was a symptom of having grown up surrounded by nothing but liars.

Soon after the murders, and after finally being able to open up to Vincent about what had happened, Prudence had been kept in the psych ward for seven excruciating months, locked down tight and far away from everyone. She was like a shell during that time, devoid of life and purpose. The only thing keeping her sane, preventing her from spiraling down a dark pit of despair, was Vincent and what he had uncovered.

My name is Demi Callard, she would remind herself. *I have to get better if I'm ever going to meet my parents.*

What she had done was so horrible that it was clear that if the truth got out, the prison would face dire consequences for its apparent gross negligence. Then came the accusations from other inmates about Benitez. It was an absolute shitstorm the prison would not likely get away from without being completely covered in it. Then came the pandemic and an offer she could not refuse.

Now Prudence sat on the bed, legs crossed with the laptop in front of her, patiently waiting for Osiris to join their meeting. Once their session was over, she and Vincent would leave for his mother's house. She had a new mixture of feelings about this: apprehension and excitement. Excited because she was enormously interested in meeting the woman who had raised one of the very few people she adored in the entire world, and apprehensive over how she would be received. Vincent had told her that Nerina was privy to what Prudence had done to end up in prison as well as the history of her childhood. Prudence could only hope that, with this knowledge, Nerina would meet her with compassion. However, she knew this might be unlikely.

"Good evening, Prudence!" Osiris' voice boomed from the speakers.

"Good evening to you as well, Osiris," Prudence replied with a smile.

"Mashallah! You are glowing today!" he exclaimed, his perfectly straight teeth on display. "Things must be going well?"

Prudence blushed, her smile widening. "Yes, very well. Yesterday, Vincent and I sold the furniture I had in storage. We had a great run this morning, and I was visited by a friend this afternoon. Oh, and tonight I'm meeting Vincent's mother, Nerina."

Osiris laughed in his deep chortle, apparently pleased with her. Prudence felt a jolt of pride. "Good, good, good. Tell me how you feel about meeting Nerina."

"I think I feel fine. I hope she likes me," Prudence confessed.

"What would her approval mean to you?"

Approval?

Prudence hadn't necessarily considered wanting her approval, but all of a sudden, she thought maybe she did want it. Perhaps even needed it.

"I suppose it would mean a great deal to me. My relationship with Vincent, though undefined, has grown a lot in the last month.

And considering how close he and his mother are, I... I think I do want her to accept me."

Osiris nodded, the lights in his office reflecting off his round spectacles. "Do you worry if she does not accept you that you might lose what you've built with Vincent?"

A solid rock saturated with fear sank in her stomach. Vincent had grown to mean so much to her that she couldn't fathom a life without him.

"Yes," she confirmed. "I really do. But... I wouldn't want him to forsake his relationship with her either."

"Hm. Elaborate on that."

"I—well, I have no way of knowing what it was like growing up in a stable, loving environment like he did. I murdered my parents for all the disgusting and vile things they forced me to endure, so to have an attachment, an unconditional love for one's parents that is reciprocated is completely foreign to me. And yet... I find I can empathize with what that might mean for him. I wouldn't want him to feel he needed to choose between us."

Osiris clasped his hands together, a slight smirk on his face. "I am very proud of you, Prudence, for coming to this conclusion and for garnering the capacity for such compassion. Understanding your own feelings has been a struggle of yours, so it is quite monumental for you to develop the ability of empathy in regards to another's feelings."

"Yes, thank you." She smiled.

"So, tonight when you meet Nerina, present yourself to her as you are. People typically have a good sense of when they are being shown something false, so you cannot pretend to be what you *think* she wants to see," Osiris said.

Prudence fidgeted with her nails. "Even though who I am is capable of monstrous things?"

"That is true, but so are we all," he said. "The sins of your past do not define who you are, especially now that you have atoned for them. This woman I see before me has blossomed, day by day, petal by petal, slowly opening up into a dazzling rose that was too long shut up in the dark. Now that the light is shining upon you and you are free to be who you've always been, you must allow yourself grace!"

He was right. She wasn't a monster, never really had been. When she killed, it had always felt like a necessity for her own self-preservation.

In truth, she had enjoyed it.

But that could have been only because she was killing people who had hurt her in some way.

What about Gretchen?

She was atoning for that. And besides, she felt great. She felt genuine joy here with Vincent. She was playful and expressive, motivated. She wanted human connection, friendships... love.

Was this the Demi she had been waiting to see?

Was this who Demi—who *she*—was meant to be?

◆

Once Prudence's session with Osiris ended, and before getting ready to leave, she sifted through her belongings. From the small bag of items she had brought with her from the prison, she produced the flier Vincent had given her in the psych ward. It had a picture of her as a baby with her biological parents' contact information below.

She studied their names for a moment: Andres and Justine Callard. Then she decided it was time.

Prudence logged into her email and, with the images Vincent obtained from Emma and Joy, she composed a message to Andres, her father.

Good Evening, Andres

It is difficult to know how to appropriately begin a message such as this. Though I fear you won't believe me or perhaps will react negatively, it is prudent that I say what I must.

My name is Prudence Malkin, or so I thought it was until very recently. I believe I was kidnapped as an infant by two people I thought my whole life to be my parents. They did unspeakable things to me when I was a young child, and I always wondered how they were so incapable of loving me the way a child should be loved. Much has happened over the years, including their passing.

A couple of months ago, I was shown a flier of a missing child by the name of Demi Callard, born January 16, 1993, missing since the spring of that year, with a birthmark on her temple. My birthday is January 16, 1993, and I have the very same birthmark. I do not expect it will be easy to believe, but I am of the impression that I am not, in fact, Prudence Malkin. I believe that I am Demi Callard. Your daughter.

I understand if you don't trust or believe me given the almost 30 years that have passed since you lost your child, but I am hopeful that you will. I have attached a photo of myself as a baby and then another a little older for you to make an assessment before deciding whether to respond. I do hope that you will.

Kindest Regards, Prudence

Prudence's cursor hovered over the "send" button for some time, fear wreaking havoc on her nervous system. She desperately wanted Andres to believe her, but what if he didn't?

What if he never responded, leaving her in the dark forever?

What if…

What if…

What if…

What if he does?

What if she could have the father she always wanted and always deserved?

What if he and Justine were still waiting for her? Waiting for this very message?

Prudence took a deep breath. As she released it, she hit "send."

Chapter 13

"Don't worry, it'll be fine. Just be yourself," Vincent reassured Demi as they waited for his mother to answer the door. "She's a bit of a hard ass, but don't take it personally."

Demi had told him what Osiris had said about meeting his mother, Nerina, and Vincent couldn't have agreed more with the advice. What drew him to her was who she truly was, and he did not doubt that it would be no different for his mom.

Vincent noticed Demi's shoulders relax slightly, but her fingers never stopped fidgeting. The door swung open and Vincent instinctively placed a reassuring hand on her lower back before smiling brightly at Nerina. His mother looked vibrant in a red knit sweater and slacks, with red lips and nails to match. Her silver-streaked bob was freshly trimmed, likely by their neighbor of thirty-five years, Voula, who had been cutting her hair since the late nineties. Mom had bragged to him the evening before over the phone about how people were up in arms at not being able to go to a salon to get their hair cut. Meanwhile, there she was, perfectly inhabited by the stipulations the pandemic had set upon the world.

"Come in, come in! You're letting all the air conditioning out," Nerina said, waving her hands into the house like a traffic conductor.

They quickly shuffled inside as directed, and Vincent helped Demi with her jacket. After he set their jackets on the rack by the front door, he kissed his mother on the cheek and thanked her for the invitation.

Nerina smiled at her boy only for the expression to subtly deflate as she turned to face Demi. Vincent gulped down his uncertainty. Though he had told Demi that his mother would be fine meeting her, he truly wasn't certain what she would do. Nerina had always been supportive of him and his decisions, but she made her wariness abundantly clear when it came to Demi.

"It's a pleasure to meet you," Demi said, extending her hand to Nerina. Her hand floated before her as she waited for Nerina to accept it, but his mother didn't move to do so. She just studied Demi, her eyes wandering over her shoulders, no doubt to check her posture, then her nails and hair for cleanliness. All the while, Demi stood still, indomitable.

"You look like someone," Nerina began, taking one step toward Demi, "in need of a mother's hug."

Demi blinked, confused. Her hand, which was still extended, trembled. Then Nerina closed the gap between them, took Demi's hand, and swept it behind her as she pulled Demi into her arms. Vincent watched in awe as the surprise in Demi's expression melted away. Her eyes closed and she held Nerina firmly, a light quiver tracing her bottom lip. Then, so softly he almost missed it, she whispered, "Thank you."

In a flash, Nerina pulled away with a nod and started spewing orders. She told Vincent to take down a pan she could not reach without her stool. Then she led Demi into the kitchen to help mold the falafel. When they entered the kitchen, the familiar scent of pita dough permeated his nostrils, while rice boiled on the stove. His mother had already sliced the tomato and onion and had mixed the falafel, which was ready in a bowl on the counter. Vincent walked past the cutting board, swiping a tomato slice from it and popping it into his mouth before his mom could see.

But nothing got past her.

"Vincent! You'll spoil your dinner!" she scolded him.

"Ma, you always say that, and yet I'm still *always* hungry." Vincent smirked as he retrieved the pan she asked for and set it on the stove.

Nerina clicked her tongue. "Hush, agóri, and take out the tzatziki and hummus from the fridge. Éla, Demi, wash your hands."

They both did as they were told. Then Nerina taught Demi how to mold the falafel. Demi took to the task so quickly, she was like a pro by her third falafel. It was almost identical to Nerina's.

Watching her connect with his mother was like the icing on the cake.

Demi closed her fingers around another mound of falafel and rolled it between her palms. "Nerina, I must commend you for teaching Vincent how to cook. I've never eaten so well in my life as I have now staying with him."

Nerina waved her hand dismissively. "No, it wasn't me. He is Greek. These recipes were in his blood from birth!"

Demi laughed. The sound curled around Vincent's heart and squeezed, making it hard to breathe.

"I'm certain growing up with an outstanding mother like you had a little something to do with it," Demi replied.

"Thank you," Nerina said, then paused. Thoughtfully, she turned to Demi, her horn-rimmed glasses perched at the tip of her nose. "I hope you understand that growing up without a good mother does not mean that you are not good too. I know life has not been easy for you, koukla mou. Likely, it has stunted you. But you must remember, an unripe grape gets sweet as honey, at a slow pace."

Vincent was flattening out the dough for the pita with the palm of his hand when he looked up and saw Demi freeze at Nerina's statement. She smiled nervously in response, then formed the last falafel and set it on the tray with the rest. She looked to Vincent, unsure what to say.

"Ma's right. Besides, that *woman* wasn't your real mother," he said. "I'm sure Justine is very kind and will welcome you with open arms when you do finally get to meet."

Demi walked over to the sink and washed her hands, her face unreadable. "I hope so."

Nerina clapped her manicured hands together and announced, "Well, now that the falafel is ready to cook, I will take over from here. O gios mou, take Demi out to the garden. I have more pomegranates than I know what to do with, so take a few, please."

Vincent led Demi through the back door, past the screened-in patio his father had built when Vincent was a child, and into the garden. Nerina had moved most of her plants, potted herbs, and tomato vines, as well as an assortment of flowers, into the patio area for the winter. She hadn't yet moved them back out, and Vincent was anticipating the time when she'd ask him to come by and help with the endeavor. In the garden, what had been planted into the ground was still covered in white sheets designed to shield them from the frigid wind.

Then, tucked back into a corner, was an over-thirty-year-old pomegranate tree that his mother had planted and grown herself. Her love showed in the thickness of its trunk and the bountiful fruit that hung heavy on its branches, ripe and ready for picking. Each year, the tree returned her affections by producing nearly one hundred or so fruit. Nerina gifted neighbors, family, and friends with syrups, glazes, juices, and desserts she made with the pomegranate, but the pandemic had put a swift stop to her tradition.

Several dozen pomegranates littered the ground, and the tree itself seemed to struggle with the weight of its unpicked fruit.

"I had no idea pomegranate trees were so resilient against the cold," Demi said, looking up into the tree. This past winter had been a harsh one, so her surprise was not unfounded.

Vincent reached up and started picking off the fruit, his body responding dutifully to the chore he had carried out his entire life. He remembered how grumpy he had been about getting fully clothed and booted to pick pomegranates in the backyard only for his aggravation to dissipate the moment the juice-filled seeds popped between his teeth. "Oh, yeah, it would take much worse to kill her."

Demi picked a few alongside him, then walked back to the patio, Vincent following closely. There, they both clutched onto the fruit. He watched her admire the greenery surrounding them. "The food she prepared tonight, did she grow it all?" Demi asked.

"Most of it, yeah. All except for the chickpeas in the falafel," he replied.

"And that word she called me. Coo—cookla... I'm sorry, I must sound like an infant." Her mouth curled at one end as a blush spread over her cheeks.

"Koúkla mou. It means something like 'my beauty' in Greek," Vincent said. "Ma doesn't hand out endearments to just anyone. She must see what I see when I look at you."

Somehow, Demi's blush deepened further. "I must admit, I'm jealous. You have the most talented and wonderful mother." She smiled, her glazed eyes looking up at him. "The mystery behind your unmatched compassion and virtue has been solved."

She thought so highly of him—a great honor coming from someone as guarded as her.

Vincent shook his head as a large smile commandeered his face. Dropping the fruit, he cupped her face in his hands and kissed her. Her lips were cold to the touch, but the scorching blood running beneath his skin warmed them at once.

God, I think I love her.

◆

Dinner was immaculate.

Empty plates—once filled with falafel gyros, lemon rice, hummus, and fresh veggies—sat in front of them. Vincent almost lost his nerve and licked the damn plate, it was so good.

His mother stood and started gathering the plates. Vincent stopped her. "I got it, Ma. You relax."

"Thank you, o gios mou. While you are in the kitchen, could you grab the dessert from the fridge?" she asked, retaking her seat.

Vincent nodded, then disappeared into the kitchen and deposited the dishes into the sink, quickly rinsing off the plates to avoid his mother's wrath. She would skin him alive if she came back to find dried hummus and rice stuck to her dishes. Then, in the fridge, he spotted the dessert, and his mouth instantly watered.

He returned with it and three sets of plates and spoons. "Ma! Portokalopita? Is it my birthday?"

Nerina waved her hand at him. "I did not make it for you! It's all for Demi." Turning to Demi, she said, "It's like an orange cake. You'll *love* it."

Demi smiled ear to ear. "Thank you, Nerina, but Vincent has been very well-behaved. I think he should be allowed one small—*very* small—piece."

Vincent bowed before Demi, a chuckle rising in his chest. "Ever so gracious, your majesty." He took her hand and placed a kiss on the back of it, then returned to his seat, impatiently awaiting his slice of cake with a spoon at the ready.

His mother laughed and served the portokalopita before rising from her seat and walking toward an ornate cabinet. She opened it and pulled out a corked bottle and a few small cordial glasses. "Would you care for any port, koúkla mou?"

Demi immediately shook her head no. "Thank you, but I don't drink."

"Not a problem. You don't mind if we partake, do you?" Nerina asked, gesturing to herself and Vincent.

"Not at all. Please do."

The first bite was a citrusy heaven and the second was somehow twice as good. Vincent reveled in the taste of the lovingly made portokalopita as his mother set a glass of port beside his plate and asked, "How has work been, Vincent?"

He took a small sip of port, then shrugged. "It's been... frustrating. They have me working on a cold case from 2013. The guy was found in an alley, his face beaten to a pulp."

Both his mother and Demi recoiled, but they continued to listen as they quietly ate their dessert.

"The police were able to determine who he was from the ID in his pocket: Alexander Travis, organ donor, lives in Buffalo. Later, they found out he was an out-of-work teacher, but it got muddy after that."

Demi's fork clanked against her plate as she set it down. A sick look washed over her face.

Worried, Vincent closed his hand around hers and squeezed it gently. "I'm sorry, we don't have to talk about this."

Demi took her hand away, placing it in her lap. "No, no, it's fine. Please go on."

Vincent's brow furrowed before he continued with caution. "So, uh, the guy had no family in Maine. Couldn't find any friends he might have corresponded with out here. Nothing."

"That is just awful. Was he robbed?" Nerina asked. The inner lining of her lips, where her lipstick had worn away, was stained purple from the port.

"No, his credit cards and cash were still in his wallet. He was found and called into the police by a random woman. They didn't get her name, unfortunately, and when they traced the call, they found out she had used a pay phone. Can you believe that? I had no idea any of those relics still worked even in 2013." Vincent finished the slice of portokalopita and took a small sip of port. "There's just not a lot to go on. They found a few strands of hair on his sweater that didn't belong to him, but the murderer's DNA wasn't in the database."

With a smirk that didn't reach her eyes, Demi pushed her unfinished dessert away, clearly unable to stomach any more. A pang of guilt pinched his stomach for discussing this case in the first place and making her uncomfortable with talk of murder.

He could only imagine how triggering it must be for her.

"This is truly incredible, Nerina, but I think I might explode if I have another bite," Demi said, "Would it be too much trouble to ask for a container to take some home?"

Nerina nodded. "Of course. Vincent, grab the Tupperware and take as much as you like."

"You don't have to tell me twice," Vincent said, springing from his seat to fetch the container from the kitchen.

They thanked his mother profusely for such a wonderful dinner and then left, pomegranates and dessert in hand.

Chapter 14

December 2013

Prudence couldn't believe her eyes. Alexander Travis was standing in her living room, but how? How did he possibly know where she lived?

And *what* was he doing here?

"This is a nice place you've got. Judging by the looks of the outside, I'm surprised at how nice you were able to make it look in here," Alex said as his eyes scanned the room, his hands in his pockets. Those hands that had held fast to her waist as he took her from behind over his desk. She could still picture the "#1 Teacher" mug that had sat in front of her as he had finished on her backside.

Prudence's body responded to the memory.

No, not him. Not again.

She had still been a child and he should have rejected her advances. He was the adult in that scenario. However, like so many of the men she'd had the misfortune of meeting, her age had been of no consequence.

"What are you doing here, Alex?" Prudence asked, her tone cool and unforgiving.

He spun around, a smug expression on his face. "I needed to see you. Six years is a long time, but I was willing to wait until you had matured."

Matured. You mean until I had become legal to fuck?

"Didn't stop you back then. What difference would time make?" she replied, watching him move closer. She was not afraid. Could never again be made to feel fear by *any* man.

"Your age had nothing to do with it, Prue. It was just you. It was your beauty and the way you held yourself, your intellectual maturity—far older than you actually were." Alex's hand rose to caress her cheek. "Even now I can see the same look you gave me that day in my classroom. You still want me, don't you?"

She jerked away from his touch. *Damn my affliction.*

Her body was betraying her mind. It was enough to make her scream. Though, perhaps she could use him again. Just to do away with these wretched desires.

Then he needed to leave.

Prudence softened her facial expression and blinked slowly up at Alex. "Can I get you anything to drink?"

A smirk unfurled, revealing gleaming white teeth and too-long canines. Prudence imagined him biting her hard enough to hurt, and a thrill surged over her skin.

"Any gin?" Alex asked.

Prudence swayed her hips as she walked around him, close enough for them to touch. "No, but I do have some scotch."

"Even better."

She heard him pull out one of the chairs at her dining room table and take a seat. In the kitchen, Prudence took down a pair of glasses and the unopened bottle of scotch from the cabinet. It had been gifted to her by the law firm she had started working for a few months ago, included in a welcome basket filled with nonsense she didn't want: cookies, chocolates, etc., though the candles were nice. Clearly, they didn't hire twenty-year-olds often, as they had failed to remove the alcohol from her basket. Not that she drank much anyway, if at all.

"Ice, or do you like it neat?" Prudence asked, serving them each a generous pour.

"Neat—like your apartment." He laughed to himself.

Prudence cringed. *Jackass.*

She took a small sip of the fourteen-year-old scotch, unsure whether she would be able to stomach it. It quickly burned bitter and hot in the back of her throat. Prudence choked back a cough as she sifted through her cabinet for something to tame the fire in her glass. She settled on two sugar cubes, which she dropped into the amber liquid and crushed with a spoon. Another small sip determined that it was still not good, but tolerable.

Prudence carried the glasses to the table with one hand, pinching the lips between her fingers, while carrying the bottle with the other. She set down the bottle, her hungry eyes not leaving his, then set the glasses in front of herself before slowly pushing his across the table to him. She leaned in deep enough to give him a clear and not-so-subtle view of cleavage bursting from the snug bodice she wore. Like a starving dog, he lapped her up with his gaze.

Still so pitiful.

"Thank you," he said, lifting the glass to her. Prudence followed suit before downing the contents of her glass. Some of the small granules of sugar coated her tongue, deliciously sweet. She poured them each another glass.

"God, you look stunning," Alex began, nursing his second glass. "I didn't show up just as you were going out, did I?"

"Does it matter?" she asked, reaching her toes out underneath the table and stroking the inside of his thigh. "You're here now."

He blushed a deep pink, a nervous laugh in his throat. "That I am."

Pathetic.

She tossed back her scotch, its effects taking hold of her quickly. Mercifully so, as it would take quite a bit of inspiration to follow through with this. Prudence was still very much attracted to Alex, even more so now due to the slight stubble on his chin and the studious lines creasing his forehead. Maybe this wouldn't be so difficult after all, regardless of how much she loathed him now for what he had done to her.

Just like back then, it was clear he would let her call the shots.

Alex grew still as she traced her toes up his inner thigh, then retreated just as she got close to where he wanted her to touch him. His body quivered and his eyes grew dark as he sipped on his scotch. His honey-blond hair fell into his face and his knuckles went white as he squeezed his hand into a fist. Prudence noticed everything. The vein pulsing in his forehead, the way his chest rose and fell beneath his royal blue sweater, his throat bobbing on a nervous gulp.

She traced the path between his legs once more, this time landing home. He was engorged, pressing against the pad of her foot.

"You're ready to skip right to it, aren't you, Prue?" Alex said, breathless.

Prudence didn't answer as she rubbed him beneath the table, firm and slow. Alex braced himself, draining his glass, a hitch in his breath, only for her to pull away. With a sly smile, Prudence tucked her feet beneath her as she sat with her legs crossed and poured each of another drink.

"Still teaching at St. Joan's?" she asked, sipping slowly this time. A fog had settled over her mind.

Alex bit his lip. "No, um, I was let go."

"Let go?"

"It's complicated. How about you, track star?" he asked, clearly avoiding the question. It wouldn't surprise her if handsome, charming Mr. Travis had been caught with another minor.

The alcohol boiled in her veins.

Her vision blurred.

"I'm an accountant."

"An accountant? I've never known accountants to be as hot as you—or as young." That stupid smirk stretched across his face again. She tossed back her scotch. It was starting to get far too easy to drink. The burn felt good.

She poured another drink.

"Whoa, slow down there, tiger," Alex said, pulling the glass away from her. Prudence seethed beneath her skin. She rose from her seat and slowly stepped up to Alex. He leaned back in his seat, looking up at her expectantly.

Prudence hiked up the hem of her dress and straddled his lap. Her breasts swelled in his face, and his hands instantly found her ass. Her lips met his and, without hesitation, he plunged his tongue into her mouth. Overly eager and evidently deprived of physical interaction, he pecked and bit and licked all over her plump lips. She squirmed on top of him as he held her tighter, clearly mistaking her movement for passion.

Pathetic and a terrible kisser.

A heavy buzz swirled in her head, numbing her so sweetly. With a great deal of effort, she pulled away from the kiss and said, "Tell me, *Alex*, how did you find me?"

"It wasn't too hard." he began, squeezing her ass firmly. "The internet is an amazing resource. Once I nailed down the apartment building you lived in, I just waited until I saw you go inside. Took a few days and no short order of courage to finally come up." Alex leaned in to steal another kiss, but Prudence backed away, narrowly avoiding his lips.

She would not be fucking this man.

The image of blood running down his face flashed in her mind, exciting her like nothing else could. She blinked again and again, watching his face blur into two: one clean and the other drenched in crimson.

Prudence's heartbeat accelerated as she let Alex continue to touch and fondle wherever his hands and lips traveled over her body. He freed one of her breasts and began to suckle on her nipple. She curled her toes as the room started to spin, and a moan escaped her lips. She gave into the fantasy and began imagining his lifeless eyes looking up at her, blood soaking his golden hair, as maroon as the changing evening sky. As he continued speaking dirty nothings, his words fell on deaf ears—ears instead filled with what she imagined his screams would sound like.

Her head fell back, her eyes fluttered, and Alex held her tighter against him. Those too-long canines grazed her neck. Every one of her nerve endings tingled and she giggled in response. As Alex continued losing himself in her skin, Prudence reached behind her and grabbed his glass. He came up for air, lust lacing his expression, and looked up at her.

"Open wide," she said, holding the glass just above his mouth. Alex bit his lip and then did as he was told.

Well-behaved pathetic dog.

She poured the remainder of his scotch over his tongue. A stream of the amber liquid ran out the side of his mouth. The moment the glass was depleted, and before his eyes could reopen, Prudence smashed the glass into his face. It shattered upon impact, cutting deep into his brow, and her senses were blessed with the sound of his screams. Adrenaline permeated her body and seeped through her pores as she removed herself from his lap. Shards of glass chimed as they hit the floor.

Tink.

Tink.

Tink.

Alex pressed his palm into his gushing forehead. "I can't see! There's blood in my eyes! You fucking bitch!"

Prudence paid his insult no mind. It wouldn't matter anyway once he was dead.

She wrapped her fingers around the neck of the bottle that sat on the table, now half empty. Lifting her foot, she pressed it into his shoulder and thrust him, causing his head to hit the floor. Alex yelped.

Looking down on him now—his face just as she had imagined it—filled her with a thrill that propelled her to continue. She sat on his chest and pinned his wrists beneath her feet. Alex's legs flailed behind her to no avail. He wasn't going anywhere.

"Shh, Mr. Travis. We wouldn't want the other students to hear us, now would we?" Prudence said, laughing in his face.

"Get the fuck off of me or I'll—"

The bottle came down on his mouth, and his teeth crunched beneath the thick glass. Then again and again and again Prudence brought the bottle down on his head until the glass shattered and he stopped moving beneath her. His blood streaked over her chest and down her arms. It was warm and thick on her hands.

Prudence took in a deep breath. The metallic scent of his blood sparked in her nostrils. As it left her lungs, her body deflated along with them. The troublesome impulses that had besieged her for the last few days were gone.

All that was left was the numbness that she longed for, with a tinge of intemperance that she did not like.

"I'm never drinking again."

Chapter 15

May 2020

What if he figures it out?

He'll leave you.

He can't leave me.

He can and he should. You're a monster, Prue.

No, I'm not, I'm getting better!

Do you regret it?

No... but Alex was a bad man! I refuse *to regret killing a bad man.*

Prudence pulled herself out of the depths of her own ominous mind, silencing the treacherous voice keen on keeping her down. Instead, she focused on Vincent, who was seated across from her at his tiny table, teaching her how to properly cut and de-seed a pomegranate. They were still in their pajamas, having slept into the early afternoon after the hardy feast the night before. They had both knocked out soon after getting home and walking Broccoli, the food that stuffed their bellies acting as a sedative.

First, he cut off the stem, revealing the sections of the fruit inside, each cluster of seeds divided by pale flesh. Then, from the start of each cluster, he sliced down the outside of the pomegranate before pulling them apart over a large bowl to catch the falling seeds.

Once open, the tiny red jewels glistened beautifully beneath the light and continued to twinkle and shine as Vincent pushed his thumbs through the many columns, releasing them from the confines of the flesh and into the bowl. Prudence watched how his fingers moved through the fruit, the veins in his hands protruding with the motion, her core heating at the sight. He was firm in his hold on the tough casing, yet gentle with the juice-filled seeds so as not to cause too many of them to burst in the wake of his extraction. Even still, a light pink juice dripped over his fingers and down his forceps. Prudence's eyes glazed over and she bit her bottom lip as she squirmed in her seat.

"And that's how it's done," Vincent concluded, discarding the flesh of the pomegranate into a plastic bag. He picked up the next one and held it out along with the knife for Prudence. "You wanna try?"

Her eyes fell on the handle of the knife. She was immediately catapulted back to the very last time she had held one. It had been substantially larger and the damage it had inflicted on Gretchen was astounding.

Enough, Prudence asserted. She wanted to be in the here and now. Not back *there* ever again.

Taking the fruit and knife, she mimicked what Vincent had shown her. First, she cut open the top. Then, using the opening, she carefully sliced down each section and pushed her thumbs through the seeds, popping many more than he did. Juice covered her hands and arms.

"I'm not quite as good as you." She smiled, one dripping hand hovering over the bowl as she discarded the abused flesh into the plastic bag. Suddenly, Vincent wrapped his fist around the wrist of her juice-covered hand. Prudence looked up at him, her heart steadily pouncing into her throat and back down again. She watched as he leaned over the table and captured two of her fingers in his mouth. Without removing his gaze from hers, he sucked the pomegranate juice off each finger, nibbling their tips lightly as he went. Prudence's eyelashes hung heavy with desire, her arousal pooling between her tightly clenched thighs, soaking her panties. Her nipples tightened into sensitive peeks beneath the silky fabric of her slip.

"You're a messy girl, Demi," Vincent said with a sly smirk, knowing exactly how he affected her. He released her hand and leaned back in his seat. Prudence stood and walked around the table to him, her thighs slick as they rubbed together. She lifted the hem of her slip and straddled his lap. His hands immediately moved to her hips, kneading and squeezing the top of her ass and thighs, his thumbs getting dangerously close to her center. A soft moan escaped her throat before she trapped it between their lips in a kiss. Her tongue slid over his, tasting the sweet juice of the pomegranate he had suckled from her fingers. Vincent kissed her in return, a deep growl rumbling in his chest. One hand continued squeezing at her waist as the other lifted the front of her slip, his thumb grazing the front of her panties over her clit.

"You're so wet for me, baby," he said against her mouth. She shuddered and whimpered, not only to his touch but also to the name he had called her.

He had never called her "baby" before.

Prudence's head fell back and he kissed and licked across her neck as he continued rubbing tortuous circles around her swollen clit. She moved her hips in tandem with his motions, pressing herself firmly into his fingers, desperately needing more pressure.

"Vincent?" she asked, her voice breathy and strained.

He groaned in response.

"You... you'll never leave m-me, will you?"

He immediately pulled away, his hand ceasing its rubbing between her legs, returning to her waist, causing the ache to spread throughout her spine like an electric shock. Looking up into her eyes now, he said, "No, I never will."

"Promise?"

A wicked smile crawled across his face. His eyes were dark, drunk with need. He squeezed her waist so tightly she squealed from the sheer strength, and he ground her pussy over the length of his engorged cock through the fabric of his sweatpants. "Does it *feel* like I could go a single day without you? The way you affect me, Demi... It's not just that my body needs you and craves you, but my very soul aches when you're not near. My heart struggles to beat when you're in pain. My entire being is wholly connected to yours and I doubt I could survive without you."

Prudence couldn't catch her breath, her heart swelling to an incomprehensible capacity threatening to burst through her chest. Vincent forced her sex to drag over him once again. The bubble in her throat burst, allowing a shriek to tear through her.

"You are *mine*," he growled, "and I am yours."

She leaned back against the table, her legs spreading wider, catching his eye. Prudence reached behind her in search of the bowl of pomegranate seeds. Her hand skimmed over the knife and retracted immediately—her heart jumping up into her throat—before finding the cusp of the bowl. She retrieved a few seeds, then teased his bottom lip with her sweet-coated fingers. Vincent opened his mouth, tongue grazing her fingertips, and she placed six seeds inside. His strong jaw contracted as he bit down on the seeds, their ruby red juice no doubt erupting all over his palate. Prudence took hold of his jaw, her fingers smoothing over his beard, and plunged her tongue into his mouth to share in the sweetness of the pomegranate.

As they kissed, Vincent's hands swept beneath her ass. Then he stood, holding her against his muscled chest. Their bodies molded together as she wrapped her arms and legs around his torso. He carried her through the French doors and into the bedroom, where he laid her down among the sheets. In one swift motion, he peeled her panties off, discarding them on the floor, and took the backs of her thighs into his large hands, pushing her knees up against her shoulders. Her pussy was on full display for him now, glistening wet at her entrance and dripping down over her inner thighs. Prudence fisted the sheets beneath her and cried out as he ran his tongue from the bottom of her slit, up through her folds, and sucked her clit into his mouth. He held her firmly in place, prohibiting her from moving as he sucked at the swollen bundle of nerves at the apex of her thighs.

His tongue slashed over it again and again.

Her every nerve tingled and burst as he continued to feast, plunging his tongue deep into her pussy, then lapping away at her clit.

"You taste so fucking sweet," Vincent cooed, his hot breath dancing over her sex. Prudence begged him not to stop, pleaded, even tried to grind herself into his mouth, but his hold on her legs was so strong she barely moved.

He sat up, her juices dripping from his beard, and pulled down the waistband of his sweatpants. His beautiful cock sprang free, so engorged its veins strained beneath the velvety skin of his shaft. Retaking his hold on her thighs, he pushed them firmly against her shoulders, lifting her ass off the bed and perfectly aligning her entrance with his cock before pushing himself within her. With a sharp intake of breath, Prudence screamed. He filled her to the hilt, deeper than ever before, stretching her so fully and suddenly that the corners of her vision darkened. "Oh my *God*!"

Vincent roared as he slammed into her. The sound of his balls slapping against her ass and the feel of his tip assaulting that sweet spot deep in her pussy caused her first orgasm to build rapidly in the depths of her core. Her muscles tightened as she came, pulling a wild howl from Vincent's throat. "That's it, baby. Look how pretty you are, taking all of me."

The moment she released him, he pulled himself from within her and flipped her onto her stomach. Dutifully, Prudence propped her knees on the bed, offering herself to him from behind. She could feel the nectar of her arousal dripping down her thighs, eager for his seed to drip down them next. But instead of his cock, Vincent shoved his tongue into her cunt, lapping up her juices and fondling her clit with his fingers. This man could not get enough and she was more than happy to oblige him.

"Oh, God!" Prudence screamed, her cheek pressed firmly in the bed as she bounced up and down on his tongue.

Vincent chuckled. “Messy, messy girl indeed.”

He replaced his tongue with two thick fingers pounding out her second orgasm as he rubbed her clit. All she could do was scream over and over as her orgasm crashed down, her arousal gushing all over his fingers. She was convulsing, her legs shaking uncontrollably, but Vincent didn’t let her go just yet. He lifted her, his fingers kneading her heavy, sensitive breasts, and pressed her back up against his chest, then lowered her onto his cock. On his knees, he pumped in and out of her deep and hard, holding her upright with one arm around her and pinching her nipples through the fabric of her slip with the other.

“Fuck, I love your cock,” Prudence said, her body shaking as he went. Hitting all the right spots deep within the chasm of her sex. His cock throbbed within her at her words.

“Say it again,” Vincent demanded, his voice guttural and beastly.

“I love your cock.”

It throbbed again as he drove into her harder. Vincent pushed her down onto all fours and gripped her shoulders in his strong hands. “Louder!”

“I love your cock!” Prudence screamed. He was tearing her apart, squeezing her shoulders to the point of pain.

She loved it.

Wanted more.

Harder.

Faster.

Again and again, he slammed into her even as he began to spill his seed. With a final roar, Vincent stopped, bowing over her, thoroughly and utterly spent. Prudence lay there, the weight of him pressing her into the bed. She wanted to melt into him just like this, to curl up beneath his sweltering hot skin.

Slowly, Vincent pulled himself from inside her, her pussy now feeling raw and empty. He kissed along her shoulders where his hands had left red marks and down her back before encouraging her to turn over. Prudence looked up at him. The fire in his eyes had reduced to simmering embers as they traced the features of her face. He rubbed his palms over the expanse of her stomach, still covered by her silk slip, and pulled down the lace-lined V-neck, causing her breasts to emerge. Gently, he circled his tongue around her nipple until it pebbled beneath his touch. Then he sucked it into his mouth. Prudence took in a shuddering breath at the feel of his teeth pinching into her breast until he released her from between his lips. "Sorry, I couldn't resist."

Prudence laughed. "By all means, get your fill."

"Oh, no. I don't think I could ever get my fill of you," Vincent replied, rubbing his face between her breasts.

"Care to join me in the shower?" she asked, running her fingers through his hair. "For old time's sake?"

He winked at her with a devilish grin and said yes before getting up and finally pulling his clothes off all the way.

"Go ahead and get the shower started. I think I heard my phone ring," he said, walking stark naked through to the door to retrieve his phone. Prudence stretched, then rolled out of bed, pulling her slip over her head before continuing into the bathroom to start the shower.

"Dem?" Vincent re-emerged moments later, his tone serious.

Prudence furrowed her brow and peeked out from behind the shower curtain. "Yes?"

"Seifert called. They're going to need you to testify a week from Friday."

Prudence nodded in acknowledgment. She had known this day would come sooner rather than later. She would tell the court what had happened, sprinkling in a few lies, and then she'd be free. Free to be with Vincent and have a chance at a normal life. Though she hated it, she could lie for him.

Would lie for him.

It was for the best.

CHAPTER 16

Prudence bathed Vincent beneath the steaming hot water. She caressed him gently as he had done for her many months ago in the showers of solitary. It felt more like centuries than months as she considered where she was now, not only physically but also mentally.

Who she was becoming.

Here she found herself caring for another as deeply as she cared for herself. Prudence wanted Vincent to feel as wanted and protected—*as loved*—as he made her feel. With the sudsy loofah, she scrubbed every inch of his skin, carefully and thoroughly. She even washed his hair and beard, her nails scratching between the many strands of his luscious and thick hair. The effect was so intimate and close, she was tempted to take him again, but refrained with a great deal of effort. He was still, his eyes closed beneath her touch, transforming into the statue of a god that she had always envisioned him to be. Chiseled, refined, smooth as silk yet hard as Parian marble. Strikingly beautiful in a way that could make any man fall to his knees in worship.

And he is mine.

After they were both scrubbed clean and dried, Vincent left the room for Prudence's session with Osiris. He told her he was planning on inviting Gallagher to come by and asked if that would be alright with her. Prudence didn't mind in the least and told him so.

In their session, she told Osiris about dinner at Nerina's and the email she had sent to Andres. In typical Osiris fashion, his sticky-sweet pride oozed through the screen of the laptop and properly coated her like a glazed sweet potato. He gushed about how proud he was of her and told her not to fret about Andres' response, as her having taken that step was a win all its own. She agreed, but the dread of his response remained, looming heavily over her.

His rejection could break her, unraveling all the work she had done. The damage, she feared, would be irreparable.

When their hour ended, Prudence closed the video chat. Instead of shutting the laptop down, she decided to check her email. Ripping off the proverbial Band-Aid, she took in a deep breath and, on the exhale, logged in. To her surprise, a message awaited her in her inbox. Her finger trembled as she clicked to open it.

```
Please call me.

-Andres Callard
```

Beneath his signature was a phone number.

It felt like the wind had been knocked from her lungs as she stared at the screen, unmoving.

Prue, you have to call him!

But what if he's angry with me for reaching out? What if he reprimands me, then rejects me?

Despite her agonizing doubt, she stood and went to the door. She peeked out at Vincent, who was sifting through a file at the kitchen island—presumably Alex's file.

Her stomach flipped, bile threatening her throat.

Fuck, it's too much.

No! Get that phone!

She called out to him with a strained squeak in her voice. "Vincent? Could I borrow your phone please?"

There was no masking the disquiet in her expression as his eyes snapped over to her. His brow furrowed and though he was slightly alarmed, Vincent walked over, pulled the cellphone out of the pocket of his sweatpants, and handed it to her. "Is everything alright?"

She nodded, unable to produce words let alone an explanation beyond that. Still fighting back the vomit searing her esophagus, she descended into the bedroom.

No, no, no, what if he isn't your father?

Prudence's stomach hollowed out as she typed in his phone number.

What if you're wrong?

Her thumb trembled over the "call" button.

But my God, Prue, what if you're right?

She pressed down and brought the phone to her ear.

It rang for what felt like an eternity. Her insides squirmed like a thousand writhing earthworms tightly packed in a dirt-filled jar. Perspiration beaded along her hairline. Her breathing was strained.

When he finally answered, she froze.

"Hello?" Andres repeated, his voice deep and raspy.

"Good evening," Prudence finally managed to say, her throat dry. "My name is Prudence Malkin. I received your email requesting that I call."

There was a pause and for a moment she contemplated throwing the phone and collapsing in on herself, but then he spoke again.

"Hey, sweetie." His words curled around a smile. The way he said "sweetie" struck something deep in her subconscious, something in her mind that recognized that exact term of endearment coupled with that particular voice.

Tears lined her eyes.

"Hey." Her voice cracked. "How are you?"

"How am I? Why, I am over the moon! I am speaking to my daughter! *My* daughter—oh my God." Andres' voice shook with a sob. "Damn it, I wish your mom hadn't just left for the store."

"My mom? How—I'm sorry, sir, but how can you be so sure that I'm her? That I'm Demi?" She hated to ask, knowing in her heart that it had to be true, but she had to.

"Sweetie, I knew the moment I laid eyes on the pictures you sent me that it was really, *really* you! You look just like me—there's no denying that. And those pictures of you as a child. I-it has to be you!" He stumbled and skipped over his words, his joy uncontainable. "Now, there is a DNA kit I'd like to send to you, only so we can be absolutely sure, but there is no doubt in my mind that you are ours."

"No, of course, I'll gladly take it." Prudence began replying to his email with Vincent's address. "I just emailed my information to you. You can send the kit there."

"Fantastic! The second we hang up, I'll take care of it. Once you take it and send it back, the results can take a few days to come in," Andres explained. "I just got your email. You're in Maine?"

"Yes, well, I hadn't always been. I was raised in New York," she replied.

"Wow... So close all these years." She could hear the shift in his voice, a stale yet ever-present sadness that must have been slowly eating away at him for the last few decades. "I don't want to wait for the test to come back. When can we meet you?"

Tears streamed silently down her face, her elation demanding to be set free, but her fear kept it down. It stomped down on her joy with the heel of it's spiked boot, mashing it deep into the trenches of her wounded heart until it seeped through the cracks of the tender seams. She hated the fear, hated it for not allowing her to express just how she was feeling in this moment.

It was the same fear that had kept her docile with Sam and Lara. The same fear that had driven her to commit unspeakable acts. The fear that had kept her in a perpetual chokehold, just out of reach of the normalcy she so desperately craved.

Fuck fear, fuck uncertainty, fuck it all!

"As soon as possible!"

Through tears and laughter laced with relief, they planned on meeting at the end of the week.

Four days.

Just four more days. Then she could be reunited with her birth parents.

CHAPTER 17

After she retrieved his phone, Vincent watched Demi shut the door behind her. He was worried and perplexed by her strange behavior and had started for the bedroom to see what was happening when a knock sounded on the door.

I'm sure everything is ok, he thought, stopping himself from entering the room. *Maybe she just wanted to call Gerty.*

It had been a few days since Demi had last spoken to Gerty. Perhaps she just needed another woman to console her after what Vincent assumed had been a rather strenuous therapy session. He acknowledged that he could not be everything she needed and was grateful to Gerty for providing the friendship and comfort that someone like Demi never had.

Brocc was scratching at the front door, whimpering and barking for his Uncle Joe to be let in. Vincent shooed him out of the way with his foot to avoid hitting him with the door as he opened it. Gallagher swung his arms around Vincent and squeezed him tightly, beer in hand, before walking inside.

"How are you, Vin?" he asked, kneeling to give Brocc the attention he required.

"Fine. Fine—great even," Vincent replied, biting his lip in an attempt to hide a smile. He wanted to shout from the rooftops about how enamored he was with Demi, how far they had come, but he feared his vocalizing these things would only backfire. As if this admission would cause a ripple effect that catapulted them back to a time when Demi was Prudence, a stone-cold siren devoid of feeling, and he was viciously fighting against her spell.

They were *so* much more than that now.

So he turned away from Gallagher to hide his eager expression and walked into the kitchen to retrieve a pair of chilled mugs from his freezer and a stout from the fridge. Gallagher followed and pulled out a single bottle from his six-pack before putting the rest in the fridge. Vincent slid one of the mugs over to him.

"Great, huh?" Gallagher winked.

Vincent shoved him lightly and poured his stout.

Leaning against the counter and sipping his Belgian white ale, Gallagher studied his friend. Vincent cringed when a knowing smirk spread across his face. "Yeah, I know what *great* means."

"Shut up, man." Vincent shook his head, taking a small sip from his beer.

"How's Dem?" Gallagher asked, looking around. "Where is she?"

Vincent gestured to the bedroom, then walked into the living room. "She's on the phone with Gerty, I think. Seems like her therapy session today was a lot, but other than that, she's been... incredible."

Still leaning against the counter in the kitchen, Gallagher asked, "So she's actually opening up now?"

"Yeah, she is! And to more than me. She met Ma yesterday. Joe, I was *stunned* by how quickly they clicked. Ma taught her how to roll falafel and she helped me pick pomegranates. And at dinner she looked right at home, chatting and eating—actually eating! Not just picking at the food then turning her nose up at her plate like she used to."

Vincent couldn't stop a goofy grin from spreading across his face or hide the sheer delight that reddened his cheeks. Direct or indirect, it was evident that he was smitten.

In a show of dramatics, Gallagher sniffed the air like a bloodhound and followed his nose into the living room. Plopping on the couch beside Vincent, he sniffed his shoulder, then unleashed a resounding howl,. "Ah-ooh! I think I smell love!"

Brocc barked in response to Gallagher's howl, his nails tapping loudly on the floor as he trotted between their legs, wanting in on whatever fun he seemed to think they were having. Vincent shoved Gallagher again. "Shut the fuck up!"

"What? You *do* love her, don't you?" Gallagher prodded, that fucking smirk not budging a centimeter.

He knows. Of course he knows.

"Yeah, but I haven't told *her* that." Vincent's eyes shot to the bedroom, fearing she might be listening.

"Why the hell not?" Gallagher asked. "Now, I'm not going to lie and say I didn't see this coming. You've had those fucking goo-goo eyes for her since she walked into that cell block!"

"I don't want to do or say anything that might freak her out. Fuck, I don't know. What if, after I tell her, everything goes to shit and she regresses under the pressure of my stupid feelings for her?"

Gallagher nodded his understanding, then rustled Vincent's hair as if he were his kid brother. "I get it, Vin. I'm glad she's doing well and I know for a *fact* you're to thank for that."

"Thanks," he replied, taking a sip of his stout, full and creamy over his tongue. "The way she smiles does things to me... Ugh, and more than that, it's her mind, her sense of humor."

"What, Demi's got jokes now?" Gallagher perked up.

"Not many, but she's surprised me with a few." Vincent grinned from ear to ear. "I'm just... I'm honored to finally meet the real Demi. Fuck... I'm falling hard."

"Mazel tov, man," Gallagher said, lifting his mug to him. Vincent clicked his mug against Gallagher's and laughed.

"Enough of me. How are you?" Vincent asked, relaxing on the couch with a deep sigh of reprieve. Gallagher proceeded to tell him about the blasé day-to-day at the prison. All had been pretty quiet lately—except for Collins, but that wasn't anything new.

Presumably, however, she had kept quiet about the incident in solitary. As far as Vincent could tell from Gallagher's account, there was no speculation about the truth as to who murdered those inmates. It seemed the controversy about Benitez's actual transgressions with the inmates was slowly dying down. This could mean that when Demi testified next week, it would fly under the radar, along with everything else, as Seifert promised. Demi would be free and the prison would avoid a scandal.

Everybody would win.

Brocc sat next to Vincent's leg, lapping away at whatever spot on his hind quarters required a thorough cleaning.

"You think he swallowed his balls?" Gallagher poked fun at the pup's strained grunting noises. They were both laughing when the doors to the bedroom swung open and Demi burst through them, jumping into Vincent's lap. Gallagher lunged out of the way. Vincent's beer sloshed in his mug and Brocc took off running to avoid the commotion.

"I spoke to him!" Prudence cried, her hands planted firmly on his chest as she straddled his thighs. "I spoke to my dad!"

"Andres?" Vincent asked, stunned. She had told him that she emailed him a few days ago.

Demi nodded, smiling from ear to ear, and embraced him, causing his beer to slosh again. Through the curtain of her hair, Vincent could scarcely see Gallagher, still seated and confused as fuck, beside them. He gestured that it was ok and remained silent.

Demi pulled away, her gaze falling on Gallagher for the first time. She wiped joyful tears from her eyes. "Hi, I'm sorry. How are you?"

"Fine—*great* even." He laughed, winking at Vincent.

Prudence slid off his lap to his opposite side and faced them both. "Forgive me, I didn't mean to interrupt your visit."

"No problem. It's nice to see you so, uh, jubilant!" Gallagher said.

"What did he say?" Vincent asked, bringing her attention back to him, eager to know what had come of their conversation.

"He said he would send me a DNA test kit to be sure, but he seems to have decided for himself already. He—he thinks I'm his daughter and we've decided to meet this Sunday."

"Where? I'll come with you." Vincent would go anywhere with her, even to the edge of the world. He'd walk to the very cusp of oblivion and then dive in happily if it meant they were together.

"He sent me their address. They live in New Jersey. Would you take me?"

Vincent turned to Gallagher. "Would you watch Brocc this Sunday for me?"

"Consider it a date," Gallagher replied with ease.

Vincent turned to Demi once more. Before he could wipe the tears streaming down her face, she hugged him tightly, burying her face in his neck. Warm, sweet gratitude traced over his skin.

Chapter 18

December 2013

The scent of copper filled the air.

Copper, sweat, and musk permeated Prudence's senses and warmed her soul. The feeling of Alex's dried blood over her skin was euphoric as it flaked beneath her touch, tickling her every nerve and leaving her wanton. She was reluctant to wash it off as she watched the water jutting from her shower head, but it had to be done.

Dismembering the body was an adrenaline rush of its own—one that Prudence had not anticipated. First, she removed his clothes, neatly folding the bloodied garments and setting them off to the side. She had studied his lifeless body then, sprawled out naked on her dining room floor. His face was almost unrecognizable, with his nose completely smashed and his upper lip ripped open, showcasing broken and missing teeth. The area where his eyes had once been was a hollow, bloody pulp, with shards of glass from the broken bottle sparkling like crimson crystals in a geode.

Rage singed the inner lining of her lungs as she thought about how he had been watching her for fuck knows how long before coming up to her apartment. It wasn't enough to fuck her when she was a vulnerable teenager fresh out of the pits of hell. Now he needed to stalk her and accost her like she were merely a thing to admire and obtain.

Prudence rose to her feet with a huff and left the room to retrieve her largest kitchen knife.

Alex wasn't a large man, so slicing through his skin, fat, and muscle was a breeze with the freshly sharpened blade. It was the severing of his bones that took some effort.

Fortunately, much like butchering a raw chicken, she found that slicing just right through the cartilage in the joints proved most effective and clean. First the right leg, then the left, both taking a total of around forty-five minutes to achieve.

Blood drained from his body and encased her legs as she knelt on the floor as close to the corpse as possible. It seeped from him slowly as it cooled and congealed.

Sticky between her fingers.

Next, she started on his arms, slicing up through the armpit and filleting his shoulders to reveal the ball and socket joint beneath the connective tissue. Prudence laid his arm flat, sawed the knife directly between the humerus and scapula, then placed the palm of her opposite hand on top of the flat side of the blade. With all her weight, she pushed down on the blade once, then another time, before it snapped through. The gratifying sound of his bones separating, the crunch beneath her hand, caused a satisfied smile to bloom across her face.

She felt proud at how well she was executing the task—her first dismemberment.

First and last, right, Prue?

She nodded, acknowledging the voice in her head. As invigorating as this was, she had no intention of killing again. No matter how much they might deserve it.

Crunch!

His other arm rolled away from the now limbless torso. Prudence set it beside his other limbs, a neat row next to his clothes, then sliced through the flesh of his throat. She sawed down until her blade met bone, then maneuvered his neck until she had cut all the way around, exposing his spine. With some effort, she cradled the nearly decapitated head in her hand as she heaved the torso upright with the other.

Prudence had heard somewhere—perhaps in a John Fowles novel—that if you twisted a human head completely around enough times, it should easily pop off. She figured, considering she had already severed the skin, muscle, and tendons, that this should be effortless. She balanced the hips of the torso between her knees and arched her back, the body's chest pressing against hers. Then, with both hands, Prudence twisted Alex's mangled head all the way around. More thick blood seeped out of the mouth and down her forearms. A squelching suction noise followed as, to her delight, the head did, in fact, pop right off. She giggled with glee and set the head on its side next to the rest of Alex.

But she wasn't through just yet.

She pushed the torso back on the floor. The wet thud it made against the blood-coated ground resounded in her ears. Her adrenaline steadily rose as she fisted his flaccid genitals.

Men with the most audacity are always the ones with the smallest dicks.

Prudence reached for the knife and gently severed his penis and testicles from his body in one piece. Without missing a beat, she turned to his discarded head, pulled his slack jaw open a little more, and shoved the member into his mouth as far down his throat as she could without causing it to fall out the other end.

Suck on that, Mr. Travis.

The next two hours were spent arranging the pieces of his corpse into the largest luggage bag she owned. Prudence made sure to remove the travel tags. She also cleaned up the blood and glass. After bleaching the floor, she discarded the used towels into the luggage alongside him. She wiped the legs of the table clean of blood, then sanitized the top and the chairs. She scrubbed the wall behind the table, paying special attention to the baseboards in case any blood had managed to drip into its grooves and cracks. Prudence washed the knife too. She planned on donating the entire set and buying a new one. There was no way she could cook with that knife again after knowing what she had used it for.

I'm not that *crazy.*

Now all that was left to clean was herself.

Prudence disrobed and put her soiled clothes into a paper bag, then stepped slowly beneath the running water. She rinsed off as best she could, not wanting to get even a small trace of blood on her loofah, before she grabbed her soap and scrubbed. The copper scent faded, folding and withering into the floral aroma of her body wash. Like roses on a grave, the flowers masked the fragrance of death.

Her skin cooled and the fog in her mind dissipated, pulling her down from her high.

She didn't think she would kill anyone after her parents. With each passing year, though the desire to do so never wavered, she was certain she could never be brought to commit murder again. But they deserved to die. Alex, her parents. They all deserved far worse than simply being released from their Earthly form.

Her parents especially.

Flashes of that night ran through her mind like a highlight reel.

Mother's yellowed nails counting the money Prudence had made them that night.

The hard metal of the crowbar, cold within her grasp.

Father aimlessly reaching back for her, the curved tool impaled in his temple.

The crash.

So much of her life didn't make sense. Pieces of the puzzle mashed together that did not fit, while others were missing completely. Why had they done what they did? Why had she been subjected to such a life for so very long?

For eight painful years, she had been passed from man to man. Raped and tortured from the age of six, a time when she still longed for her parents' love and approval. When she was good, did as she was told, and did not cry, Father gave her what she desired. He coddled her, praised her for doing so well, and fed her sweets. He snuggled with her at night, holding her suffocatingly close. And though she could feel him grow hard behind her, and his hands wandered, she would push it from her mind so she could enjoy what little affection she got.

Mother, on the other hand, never showed her love.

She would do the basics of what a mother should do. She bought her clothes—very pretty clothes, to be sure—and dressed her up like a proper doll. She made sure Prudence was well-fed and bathed, but that was where it ended. Mother tucked her in at night only to glare at her with an unparalleled disdain as Father curled up in bed with Prudence. She scolded Prudence for being disgusting, dirty, unclean after being with those men, solidifying Prudence's own self-view.

She was unworthy filth through and through.

Once, when it all began, Prudence remembered watching Mother out of the corner of her eye as she washed the dishes. She never dared to look at her directly for fear of getting in trouble for staring.

They had just had a marvelous pancake breakfast, a rarity in their house, and Mother had spoken so sweetly to her.

Prudence wanted more of that kindness.

So she looked through her peripheral vision at Mother, pretending to pay attention to her Strawberry Shortcake coloring book. She wanted so badly to get her attention and to prolong the happiness of that morning. However, it was evident by the way Mother aggressively scrubbed the dishes and scowled that her mood was souring.

But why? I don't understand why!

She had been a good girl, or had desperately tried to be. Why couldn't Mother see that?

Why couldn't Mother see that she was trying?

Mother told her she was going to shower and that Prudence better behave while she was gone. Prudence vehemently nodded, promising that she would. But before Mother could leave the room, a knock sounded on the door. She went to answer it and quickly dove into an argument with a woman just outside. Prudence could hear the woman's voice as she bartered with Mother about a little boy she was trying to give her.

Mother called the woman "Ramona."

Curiosity got the better of Prudence as she jumped off the couch and ventured toward the door. She quietly crept behind Mother to peek outside at the woman and a boy whom Ramona called Dante. Her eyes fell on the boy first. His pale green eyes struck her, forming a stark contrast with his tawny brown skin.

He was very little—littler than her.

His face was solemn and she knew, without really knowing, exactly how he felt.

Ramona was tall and had porcelain skin splattered with an agglomeration of freckles. Her expression bore a subtle nefarious look buried beneath layers of half-truths and secrets. Prudence froze in fear at the sight of her green eyes, which speared right through her.

A fire sliced through her cheek and spread over her face as Mother's hand slapped her. Pain prickled her cheek, and tears burned as they instantly welled up in her eyes.

Fuck.

Her mind jolted back to the present. Scalding hot water cascaded down her back. Prudence wiped fresh tears from her eyes. Her hatred for Mother was fresh in the hollow, black pit of her chest. At that moment, she knew that, if given a second chance, she would kill that bitch again.

◆

A chilling breeze rushed through the back alley of a convenience store a few blocks from Prudence's apartment building. She rolled the luggage—Alex stuffed securely inside—down the narrow space between buildings and propped it against an overflowing dumpster.

This gives new meaning to the phrase "taking out the trash."

Prudence laughed quietly to herself as she grabbed the paper bag with her bloodied clothes and walked around the corner to the front of the convenience store. There, she found one of the few payphones still operational in the city. She grabbed the receiver with her gloved hands, deposited a few quarters into the coin slot, and dialed 911.

The phone was answered on the second ring. "911, what's your emergency?"

"I'm at the intersection of Cutts and Center. There's a suitcase with human remains inside by the dumpster." Prudence spoke quickly and efficiently.

"We'll dispatch an officer to you," the dispatcher replied dryly, evidently often hearing horrible things like this, judging by the lack of a reaction. "What's your name and callback number in case we get disconnected?... Hello? Hello, ma'am?"

Prudence hung up the phone, discarded her gloves in the trash can beside the pay phone, and went back home, stopping only to throw the bag of clothes in a random bin halfway there.

Chapter 19

May 2020

Few events in a person's life could be defined as pivotal. Life-altering. Events with the ability to both elevate and destroy. Once they occurred, they promptly changed the trajectory of a person's life without giving them any indication of what would come.

Marriage could end in the promises of vows fulfilled or in divorce.

Having children could result in well-rounded, healthy adults or in a traumatic disaster.

Going to college could result in a degree or in failure and regret.

Prudence had no way of knowing what to expect in the days leading up to meeting her parents. However, despite the unknown, she was filled to the brim with excitement and hope. She spoke with her father every day, usually in the morning after her and Vincent's daily run.

"So those legs of yours haven't fallen off *yet*?" Andres asked every time, in awe of her ability to get up each morning and run close to five miles.

With his raspy voice and tendency to use humor when speaking, he made her feel safe and cozy. At times, he could be gentle and thoughtful with his words when sharing something difficult or listening to Prudence's recollections of her childhood. He was anguished to learn the little she shared about being trafficked by those wretched people who had posed as her parents for all that time. She did not shy away from telling him how they had met their demise, not wanting to keep anything from him. Her past was her past and she had no intention of hiding it, even if that meant his rejection of her.

Regardless of the utter despair it would cause her, Prudence had come to understand, from a young age, that lies would only inflate and erode within her. It was a burden she refused to carry.

Andres was quiet for a moment. Then a deep breath, followed by a heavy sigh, resounded through the receiver. "Well, sweetie, it was self-defense, like they say. You had to do what you had to do to get the fuck outta there. If I'm being honest, had you not killed them, I would have done it my damn self. Those sick fucks..."

He told her about her little brother, who had passed away after accidentally drowning in the family pool at age three. Prudence's heart broke for the sibling she never knew and for the pain her parents had continued to endure after her kidnapping. How anyone was capable of surviving such cruel bouts of fate was almost unbelievable—almost considering she had also survived the unimaginable.

It made her feel so close to Justine and Andres.

Mom and Dad.

Sunday arrived with an overcast sky threatening rain. Evidently, there was to be some weather in New Jersey as well. Andres had sent Prudence the forecast and insisted that they stay the night instead of driving the five hours there and then back through rain storms all in one day. She agreed and packed an overnight bag for herself and

Vincent with a change of clothes and a few of their toiletries. She and Vincent also took the time to get tested to reassure her parents that neither of them had contracted COVID, considering they'd had visits from both Gerty and Gallagher since they were last tested. Thankfully, they both came back negative.

Vincent walked Broccoli one last time, then checked his food and water before they left. Gallagher had to work that morning but planned on coming by afterward and staying the night with Brocc.

Halfway to New Jersey, Prudence felt like she was sitting on pins and needles. Her nerves were so bad that she was shaking her leg incessantly and chewing on her inner cheek. Andres texted to inform her that the results from their DNA test had come in, but they would wait to open them until she arrived.

What if they weren't a match?

If they weren't her parents, what would she do?

What would she say?

Was this trip all for naught?

"Nervous?" Vincent asked, his even tone cutting through the tension in the air like a knife. He was so calm while she sat there coming apart at the seams. Prudence hated this feeling, hated how insecure and irritable she was.

"Extremely," she admitted, doing her best to stop shaking.

"Take off your leggings," Vincent said.

Her eyes shot to him, confusion written all over her face. "Excuse me?"

They were going seventy miles per hour on a rural highway, with stretches of trees and nothing but grassland and the occasional herd of cows on either side. He let his eyes leave the road for only a moment, a stern authority in the deep pools of his irises. "I'm not going to ask you again."

Prudence continued staring at him after he returned his gaze to the road. Chiseled, bearded jaw, muscled neck and shoulders. His straight nose with a slight bump, which she had ridden so many times at this point. She shuddered on a breath as she hooked her thumbs into the waistband of her leggings and pulled them from underneath her bottom. The seatbelt pinched at her waist as she pulled them down her legs and off her feet.

He smirked, watching her periodically through his peripheral vision. "That's my girl. Put your right leg up on the dash."

Prudence did as she was told, warmth pooling throughout her core as she bared herself to him, the sky, and any cars that might have been passing by. Her stress eddied from her mind only to be replaced by an unbridled longing.

She bit her bottom lip.

Now that she was in position, Vincent lathered his fingers over his tongue, generously coating them with saliva, then reached in between her thighs. She flinched on contact, his fingers brazenly rubbing at her clit before sliding through her folds. He teased her entrance without dipping inside. Prudence whimpered, clutching her armrest and curling her toes.

"Don't worry, baby, I've got you," he said, then pushed his middle finger inside. Her eyes rolled back in her head, her hips working against him as his finger curled inside her and retreated to circle her clit.

Prudence looked over at him. His eyes were trained on the road and his fingers were trained on her cunt.

"You're so swollen," he said, increasing his pace. She fisted the grab handle and dug the nails of her opposite hand into the fabric of the armrest as the intensity built and swelled in her center. Just as she was ready to come up over the edge, he plunged three thick fingers into her pussy. She watched the veins in his forearms bulge as he drove into her, the sounds of her overflowing juices driving her to an increasingly dangerous heat.

He couldn't fathom what he did to her, the limits he brought her to. The astronomical levels of intoxication she felt.

This is insane, she thought as he destroyed her pussy with his fingers. Trees wiped past them in a blur as her back pressed more firmly against the seat and her heart pounded in her chest. Prudence wept quietly as she took it, his thumb assaulting her clit all the while.

She was coming, *fuck*, she was coming.

"Let go, baby." Her pussy clenched tightly around his fingers. "Let go, I've got you."

She arched her back and let out a scream as she came hard. He pulled fingers from within the chasm of her sex and then licked them clean, a satisfied grumble rolling in his chest. With heat still permeating her core, Prudence unbuckled her seat belt and lunged over. Bare ass up, she unbuttoned and unzipped his pants. The moment she held his rock-hard cock in her hands, Vincent wrapped her curls around his fist and pulled, keeping her tongue just out of reach of him.

"Beg for it," he demanded through clenched teeth.

"Please." Her voice trembled as her hand gripped him more firmly. "Please let me suck your cock, Vincent."

There was a low rumble in his chest. Then he set the cruise control and removed his foot from the gas.

"Look at me," he said, so she did. "Open your mouth."

With her large eyes piercing his, she opened her mouth wide and stuck out her tongue, eager to receive him. Vincent released his hold on her locks and she swiftly took him to the back of her throat. He groaned loudly, reaching over to smack her ass hard. She gargled a squeal over his cock, then sucked him faster, taking his length all the way down.

He gripped the back of her neck to temper her. "No, go slow. I want to feel you."

She didn't want to go slow. She wanted to devour him just as he had done to her, but she would submit and do whatever he liked with no questions asked. Squeezing his thigh and the base of his cock, she slowed down, languidly running her tongue up and down his shaft. She drooled all over his cock and used it to pump his erection as she paid special attention to the tip.

Vincent peeked down at her for a moment, his cock throbbing in her hand. "Ah, *fuck*. Do you feel what you do to me?"

Prudence smiled, her tongue flicking the head. Vincent reached over, running his hand over her ass, and plunged his fingers into her from behind. She was sopping wet and a moan erupted from within her at how he filled her up again. He swerved the truck, too heavily distracted. Vincent corrected the wheel but kept his fingers circling deep inside her pussy. "Look at the mess you're making."

Prudence couldn't hold back anymore.

She sucked him in hard, pushing him so far down her throat that she gagged and cut off her airway. Again and again she pushed, feeling his orgasm and hers rising within them.

"I'm about to come, baby," he warned, but Prudence did not relent as her body again rolled with her climax. When she took him deep once more, her throat was met with ropes of his cum shooting down her esophagus. Once he was spent, she released his cock and sat up, licking her lips free of the salty substance.

Vincent zipped himself back up, his breathing labored as he regained his equilibrium. Prudence pulled her leggings on and slumped back in her seat, thoroughly spent.

"Feel a little better?" Vincent asked.

Prudence giggled. "Oh, Officer Kore. Each day you prove more and more why you're the only one for me."

He smiled ear to ear as he took the truck off cruise control and returned his foot to the gas. "Good, because I have a strict no-return policy. You won't be getting rid of me, Dem."

CHAPTER 20

Thunder rolled as Vincent drove them into the driveway of a quaint family-style home in a suburb of Glassboro, New Jersey. They had been lucky to have missed the rain, but now it seemed the storm clouds had found them. Just as the sky opened up its maw to rain down upon them, Prudence and Vincent scurried to the front door. Prudence located the doorbell and, with a trembling finger, pressed the button. Bells tolled on the other side of the door, echoing off the walls of the house's interior. The sound of the rain behind their backs died with the swelling bedlam inside her chest.

Her heart pounded in her ears, while her breath came in quick, uneven pants.

Vincent wrapped his arm around her middle and pulled her back against his solid chest. With a kiss on the top of her head, he was able to steady her heart. She took in a breath that extended low into her lungs like roots. On the exhale, the door swung open.

Prudence's eyes locked on a pair that mirrored her own. They were depthless, dark brown eyes like bowls of decadent melted chocolate. Those eyes like hers were set in an equally dark face. Andres' skin was a rich and complex umber, his lips full like hers. His jaw was a more squared variation of hers with gray and white whiskers growing from it in coarse strands.

Finally, a puzzle piece that fit.

Now it made sense why her skin had always been darker than Sam and Lara's as she gazed into the face of the Black man who must have fathered her.

He smiled the widest, most infectious smile she had ever seen, and her heart bounced against her rib cage blissfully at the sight. Andres opened his arms and closed the space between them, scooping her into a warm embrace. He easily lifted her off the ground with his tall frame and swung her around like a child, his ashy laugh revitalizing. He smelled like citrus and smoked cedar.

"Hello, my beautiful daughter!" Andres said, setting her back down. He noticed Vincent and shook his hand excitedly. "A pleasure to meet you too, Vincent! Thank you for bringing my baby back to me."

"No, sir, the pleasure is all mine," Vincent replied.

Andres walked back into the house and waved them inside. It was warm and the walls were adorned with family photos and paintings. The tile floor was draped in a soft runner leading down the hallway, which they took deeper into the house.

"Justine! Our daughter is here!"

Another electric jolt of elation shot through Prudence. She took Vincent's hand for support, fearing she'd faint from all the excitement. The aroma of seafood and fresh dill filled the air, making her stomach growl. Andres walked them into the dining room, where four place settings were arranged neatly on a hardwood table. Then Prudence's eyes fell on an envelope.

Andres picked it up and her heart stopped.

"I'm sorry, but now that I've seen you, I can't wait a second longer. Would you do the honors?" he asked, handing the sealed parcel to Prudence. "Justine!"

"I'm getting the salmon out of the oven before it dries out," she called from what Prudence assumed was the kitchen. Justine's voice, like Andres', was so familiar that it made Prudence's heart cheer even louder. "Go on, don't wait on me!"

Andres dramatically rolled his eyes. "I swear, that woman will be late to her own funeral. Go on, open it!"

Prudence laughed nervously at his joke, then looked down at her fingers, which held the defining factor to her existence. She shook her head and handed it to Vincent. "I can't, I'm... afraid," she admitted, her gaze pleading for his help.

Vincent took it from her and squeezed her hand reassuringly before letting her go. "Don't worry, baby, I've got you." His words from earlier took on a new meaning. It was evident that he would always have her in every context, and for that she was deeply grateful.

Vincent tore open the envelope and removed its contents. As his eyes skimmed over the page, his brow softened and his lips curled into a grin. "Andres, you are the father."

Andres howled and his arms shot up high. "Yes! I knew it! I knew it had to be you!"

Relief cooled Prudence's skin as she allowed herself to laugh and cheer along with him, hugging him and spinning around and around.

"Is she really?" Prudence heard Justine's voice behind her as she entered the room. "Is she really our Demi?"

Prudence whirled around, beaming from ear to ear, ready to retrieve another long-lost piece of the puzzle, when she saw her mother standing there holding a Pyrex dish. Prudence's heart dropped into her stomach, fizzing and breaking apart into nothing like an alkaline brick. Her smile melted and her eyes widened.

Justine's porcelain skin was covered in freckles.

Her hair was bone-straight over her shoulders.

Her green eyes were piercing.

Through bile swelling up in her throat, Prudence barely managed a whisper. "Ramona?"

Justine faltered ever so subtly. Her brow twitched and her smile flattened for a fraction of a second before she regained her composure. She laughed, setting the salmon dish in the center of the table. "Ramona? No, my name is Justine."

Vincent stepped toward her, clearly unsure what was happening. "Dem, who's Ramona?"

But she ignored him as her fury sent a flame through her body. Andres cupped Prudence's shoulder, pulling her against him, having missed his wife's slipped mask. He was likely still elated by the results, unable to be brought down from his cloud.

How she wished to be brought back to her cloud, where the joy could blind her from the truth.

"I hope you like salmon. Your mom makes it with fresh dill and sliced lemon," Andres told her, pointing at the crispy pink fish on the table, neatly placed on top of a bed of rice pilaf and parsnips. Prudence shook out of his grasp and backed away from them all. "No, no, I *remember* you," she said, pointing at her mother.

Justine laughed again, less genuinely this time.

It sounded more like a warning.

"There's no way. You were only a few months old when you were *taken* from us." She folded her arms, clearly trying to maintain a look of disbelief.

Prudence could see through her ruse. "You're right," she said, straightening her spine and looking down at Justine from the tip of her nose. She could feel Vincent's and Andres' eyes on her. The room grew still. "And then I was six when I saw you again."

"Hold on, wait a minute." Andres stepped between the two women. "What is she saying, Justine?"

Justine's glare shifted from Prudence to her husband. His expression was filled with hurt and confusion. It looked like she tried to soften her gaze but failed, saying nothing to him in return. Instead, she scoffed and glared at him.

"Mother called you Ramona that day," Prudence said, drawing everyone's attention back to her. "I remember your eyes, the disgusted look in them when they fell on *me*." Prudence clenched her fists. "And the boy... the boy."

Andres swallowed hard. "What boy?"

Prudence struggled to find the boy in the caverns of her mind. His tawny face and emerald green eyes resurfaced, a corpse coming up through murky waters and bobbing up to the shoal of her memory. "Dante. His name was Dante."

The realization of who he could be struck her like a lightning bolt to the skull. She felt like she might vomit when she asked, "That little boy, was he—was he my brother?"

"I don't have time for this," Justine said through clenched teeth. "Clearly she's insane, Andres!"

"He was, wasn't he? You tried to sell my brother to them too. Then, when they wouldn't take him, you..." Prudence's voice trembled and her clenched fists shook at her sides. It was all so clear, the puzzle pieces coming together seemingly on their own. "He didn't accidentally drown, did he, Ramona—or Justine or whatever the fuck your name is! It wasn't an accident, was it? Was it!"

Andres' eyes widened in terror. Justine gasped as if she were mortified by the allegation. She was a class-A manipulator. Prudence was all too familiar with her type.

"How dare you make such accusations!" Justine shrieked, stomping her foot. "Andres, can you believe what she's saying about me?"

"Tell the truth!" Prudence screamed. "You threw me to the fucking wolves as an infant knowing what would happen to me. Knowing I would be beaten and fucked and held captive like a damn rat in a lab to be used and abused and then discarded when I finally succumbed to the torture!"

Justine was simmering with rage. "Get out of my house!"

"You saw me that day and saw the way Lara slapped me," Prudence continued, stepping closer. Adrenaline pumped in her ears.

"You saw the bruises on my body and did nothing! Then you tried to give Dante to them. Your fucking children! You cultivated me in your womb, nourished me into life, held me in your arms, and then threw me away like trash!"

"Demi," Vincent said, walking closer with his hands reaching out for her—a line, a branch, a tether to bring her back to safety.

She didn't take it.

"Andres, are you seriously going to stand there and let this girl talk to me—your *wife*—this way?" Justine's shrill voice heightened Prudence's heart rate.

She wanted to rip the woman's vocal cords out of her fucking throat. "Tell the truth!"

Tears cascaded down Andres' cheeks as he gazed hopelessly at his wife, his partner, the mother of his children. "Why?"

Justine's eyes widened and she bared her teeth like a wild animal. "Why *what*? You don't believe her, do you? Over me? Me, who has fought just as hard as you to find her? Who found our darling son face down in the pool that horrible, awful day?"

"I never told Demi—" Andres began when a sob crashed over him. His hands shook as he brought them to his face. Lighting struck, flashing through the window, to be followed by a clap of thunder. The rain beat loudly on the roof of the house, equaling the rage that roared within Prudence's head.

"What?" Justine snapped impatiently, her hands on her hips. "You never told her what?"

"His name, Justine! I never told her Dante's name."

Justine was dumbstruck. Her knees wobbled as she took a step back like she might retreat.

Prudence charged toward her. "I knew it! You are the Devil incarnate!"

"*I'm* the Devil? If that's true then the apple doesn't fall too far from the tree, *Prudence*. Killing that poor woman and going to prison for it. Bet you didn't tell your father that!" Justine raged. The mask had come off completely, falling to the floor and revealing the hellion beneath the façade—that nefarious face filled with deception out on display for all to see. "I made the right choice giving you up. If I hadn't, you would have killed us too. I could tell you were a bad seed from the start."

Prudence grabbed the still piping hot dish from the table, hardly registering how it singed her fingertips, and smashed it at Justine's feet. Ceramic shards flew left and right, hot grains of rice peppered their legs and the floor. The filet of fish fell apart, parsnips rolling away. Vincent and Andres jumped back and Justine screamed. Her rage that should have been for what happened to her own flesh and blood displaced and instead conjured up for the lovely meal she had prepared.

"I wouldn't be like this if you hadn't thrown me away!" Prudence said. "You're to blame for *everything* that happened to me and *everything* that I have become!"

Justine stepped over the mess on the floor, salmon smooshing beneath her sandals, and got right into Prudence's face. "If Andres hadn't wanted you so badly, I would have aborted you the moment I learned I was pregnant! You filthy, heinous little bitch!"

Prudence screamed, slashing her nails at Justine, trying to grab her by the throat. Trying to strangle her until the light faded from her eyes. Vincent pulled her back just in time. She tore away from him and took off running to the front door, then out of the house. Andres and Vincent called after her, but she ignored them, allowing the pouring rain to consume her as she bolted down the street.

Prudence pushed herself harder, running faster as the rain pelted her skin, drenching her from head to toe. Lightning illuminated the sky, its jagged bolts spreading like the claw of God reaching down to smite her.

This was his payment to her for all her sins.

This final betrayal.

Are you not the same God who allowed all this?

Are you not the same God who stood idly by while grown men defiled my prepubescent body?

Are you not the same God who ignored my prayers and my cries for help?

You are no God of mine.

I smite you in my own name. I denounce you from the kingdom of heaven, for you are no worthy God!

She heard footsteps behind her. Prudence tried to keep going, but arms folded around her and scooped her up against a muscled chest that she knew so well.

"No! Put me down, Vincent!" she screamed, bucking against him, thrashing to get away.

But he refused.

Vincent shifted her body in his grasp, draping her legs over one arm and supporting her back with the other.

"I've got you, Dem," he said, walking them back to his truck.

Prudence wailed in anguish, fisting his soaked sweater. She begged for death to find her and drag her dilapidated body down into the underworld where she belonged. She would rather drown for eternity in the river of souls below than carry on living with the knowledge that her own mother was the one who had damned her.

Chapter 21

The entire ride back to Maine was silent. Demi stared out the window, unmoving, tears streaming down her face, until she fell asleep. When Vincent stopped for gas and asked if she would like any refreshments or to use the restroom, she did not reply or even move to indicate that she had heard him. He bought her a bottle of water anyway, but it sat untouched in the cup holder.

So much had happened in the few minutes they spent at the Callard home that Vincent was having trouble wrapping his mind around it all. What had started as a beautiful, heartfelt reunion soured when Justine entered the room.

She appeared sweet, holding their dinner with her periwinkle oven mitts. Her hair was nice and neat over her shoulders and light in color. Her clothes appeared freshly laundered, the crisp white capris pleated down the front and her button-up pale blue blouse stiff with starch. She seemed like an ordinary older woman. Then Demi had called her mother by a different name, a name she had not mentioned to him before.

Ramona.

He had watched Demi go from rejoicing and cheering with her father Andres to weary and volatile. Her body had gone into defensive mode, like a cat arching its back and flattening its ears. She had folded and erected a wall around her, her eyes shifting, her lips curled down. Vincent had been taken aback by her demeanor and had tried to take a step toward her, but something about her had set off warning bells in his head, telling him to keep his distance. This feeling left a bitter taste on his tongue.

Something was horribly wrong.

Then Demi had accused Justine of giving her away and having something to do with her brother's death. He couldn't believe what he was hearing. To think a mother would knowingly sell her child to be a sex slave, then attempt to do so again with her second child, made him sick to his stomach. But it had to be true, as Demi did not lie. She had not always been the most forthcoming about things, but she never, ever lied.

Despite the rage that simmered off her, and the fear of her lashing out at him too, Vincent had called for her and reached out his hand for her to take. He had wanted so desperately to console her and let her know that he was still there. That even if everyone in the world turned against her, he never would. He had pleaded with his eyes, his arms trembling as if he were reaching out to a hostile dog with its teeth bared. But she had not relented. Her rejection of him had stung more than he cared to admit, but he tried not to think about his own feelings at that moment.

It was her world that was falling apart, after all.

And then, Andres' revelation that he had not told her their late son's name confirmed that Demi had been telling the truth. Justine—or Ramona, as Demi had called her—was responsible for her disappearance and, quite possibly, Dante's demise.

When Justine had thrown those contemptuous insults at Demi, Vincent had wanted to tear the whole house apart—and would have had Demi not taken off the way she did. He couldn't risk losing her, couldn't let her be alone after all that had transpired, so he had gone after her without another word to her parents.

After they had left, Vincent had seen notifications go off repeatedly on his phone as Andres texted and called. Though it was evident that Andres had been completely in the dark about what his wife had done, Vincent didn't answer any of them. He decided it wasn't his place and that he would give Demi the option to respond or not—just not right away.

When they finally got home, it was almost ten o'clock at night. Gallagher was still up watching cartoons with Brocc snoring in his lap when Vincent and Demi walked through the door.

"Hey!" Gallagher greeted them. "I wasn't expecting you two until tomorrow. How'd it go?"

Demi made a beeline for the bedroom and shut the door. Vincent set their bag by the island with a somber expression on his face.

Gallagher looked from him to the bedroom door, his brow furrowing. "Vin, what happened?"

Vincent sighed and rubbed the back of his neck, "I—uh. We'll have to talk about it later."

Gallagher shut off the television, removed Brocc from his lap, and walked over to Vincent, "No problem, I'll head out. Call me if either of you need anything, alright?"

"I will. Thanks, man."

Gallagher hugged him and patted him hard on the back before taking his overnight bag and leaving.

Vincent stood quietly for a moment in the kitchen. The apartment was eerily still except for Brocc's breathing and the hum of the heater as it struggled to keep up with the frigid temperatures outside. He walked to the bedroom door and stood just outside, hesitant to enter. Listening intently, he heard a faint whimper coming from inside. His heart broke further for Demi.

His Demi.

He couldn't leave her to cry and endure her grief without the comfort and care of someone who truly and deeply loved her. Vincent opened the door and stepped inside to find her curled up on the bed. Her shoulders shook from her quiet sobs and hiccups. He walked around the bed and knelt in front of her. Her curls were draped over her face, her knees were pulled into her chest, and she gripped the pillow beneath her head. Vincent smoothed her hair out of the way to reveal tear-stained cheeks and a rosy nose. Her eyes were bloodshot and her lip quivered, but her features softened at the sight of him. Her lip ceased its quivering and pouted instead, full and delicious. Her eyes—once filled with sorrow—filled with something more akin to desire.

"Are you ok?" he asked, taking her hand and rubbing the back of it with his thumb. Her gaze trailed down to his fingers, and then his chest, and then up his throat. She sat up slowly, holding his hand up and pressing it to her heart. He could feel the damaged organ flutter profusely within her chest. "What can I do for you? Would you like to talk about it? Maybe I can call Dr. Agubulom?"

Demi slowly shook her head no, a hunger growing in her stare. She caressed his jaw, her fingertips running through the soft strands of his beard. Then she leaned in and kissed him gently on the lips. Vincent closed his eyes and she kissed him again, longer this time. Then again, moving in closer, sliding his hand over her breast. He cupped it and squeezed gently, his tongue pushing past her lips. She moaned into his mouth, her hands sliding down to the hem of his sweater.

Something is off, he thought. His eyes sprang open as she attempted to lift his sweater over his head. He stopped her, grabbing her wrists. "Demi, stop. I don't think this is the right time," he said.

"No, it's exactly the right time," she replied, kissing him more assertively. She bit and sucked on his lips and lathered her tongue over them.

Vincent pushed away from her and rose to his feet. "Stop, Dem."

But she didn't listen. She frantically unfastened his jeans, wanting to have her way with him anyway. Was she trying to drown out the pain the best way she knew how? Through pleasure and meaningless sex? That could never be what they were to each other. She'd said it herself. She'd said she couldn't use him—not in this way—ever again, and yet there she was, forcing something he knew neither of them wanted right then. It was something she did not need in this moment of anguish and despair.

He wrenched up her wrists again and held her at arm's length. "No, this isn't right, Demi. We can talk about this. I... I love you."

She ripped herself from his grasp, fury contorting her features, and screamed, "I don't want you to *love* me, I want you to fuck me!"

His temple pulsed with the gnashing of his jaw and his face fell. No, this was all wrong and he could not be around her right now. Vincent stepped away from her. Then, just as quickly as the anger took hold of Demi, it faded, to be replaced with regret. In a sudden eruption of terror, she climbed out of the bed and fell to her knees before him. "No, no, no, no. I'm sorry, I'm sorry!"

Vincent shook his head and walked around her. "I've gotta go."

"Wait, no, please!" she pleaded, her voice cracking with desperation and panic.

"I just need a minute, Dem," he said firmly, his hand finding the doorknob.

A gut-wrenching cry came from within her. "Don't leave me!" Demi screamed, seeming to shake the foundation of the entire apartment building. She collapsed to the ground, her cheek flush with the floor, tears staining the hardwood beneath her. She sobbed loudly, so loudly her body shook. Her nails dug perilously at the boards. Brocc howled from the other room and whined at the closed door. Demi's sobs were so loud and all-consuming, she didn't hear Vincent's footsteps as he walked back toward her. Only when he lay on the ground beside her, wrapped himself around her, and pulled her trembling body into his did she realize he had not gone.

"I'm not leaving you, baby. Didn't you hear what I said?" he asked, his voice low and gentle, causing her body to relax beneath him.

"I said I love you. Me needing space doesn't mean I'm going to leave you."

Demi curled into him, clutching at his chest as if she would float away if she didn't grab onto something. Vincent squeezed her tightly and kissed the top of her head as he gently rocked her back and forth on the floor.

"Why didn't she want me?" she asked, her voice muffled in his sweater.

Because she's selfish?

Because she's the dumbest person alive?

Because she's the world's largest pile of steaming hot shit?

Countless reasons ran through Vincent's mind as a response but he could use none of them to answer definitively. So instead he said, "Only she knows why... But I can guarantee it was not because of anything you did, Demi."

Demi whispered, "Maybe she could see it."

"See what?" he asked, continuing to stroke her hair.

"The darkness inside me."

He shook his head and pulled away slightly so he could look her in the eyes. "No child is born with darkness inside them and you were no different. Justine and all those other bastards who used you are responsible for putting it there."

She gazed up at him, a mixture of hope and disbelief swirling in her deep, dark irises.

◆

Prudence did not leave the bed for three days.

At dawn, Vincent would bring her a small breakfast. Toast with coffee. Vanilla yogurt with pomegranate seeds, almond slivers, and a honey drizzle. Black tea alongside an egg scramble with feta, spinach, and tomato. She never ate it and he would return to a stale plate of food, which he would promptly remove from the room only to return a few hours later with more food for lunch and dinner. The same glass of water stayed at her bedside filled to the brim, untouched. She did not speak, did not acknowledge Broccoli the few times he scurried past Vincent to lick her fingertips and whine for her attention.

Worst of all, she was missing her court-ordered appointments with Osiris. He would want to discuss all that had happened, and she simply did not have the energy or life force left to divulge it all, let alone sort through the muck to make sense of it.

She didn't want it to make sense.

At night, Vincent curled up behind her and held her tightly, protecting her from the monsters that dwelled within the dark trenches of her mind. However, no matter how much comfort he brought her, how much he tried, he could not provide her with what she wanted.

She wanted Ramona dead.

Chapter 22

"Ma, I don't know what to do," Vincent confessed to Nerina over the phone. "She's been in bed all week. She's not eating or drinking anything. And with her court date coming up in two days... It's like she's trying to waste away..."

Nerina sighed the way only concerned mothers could sigh, then asked, "Have you tried encouraging her to go for a walk to get some fresh air?"

Vincent sat at his couch, his laptop open on the cold case file he had been working on, his notes sprawled on the coffee table. He had been trying, and failing, to work despite his overwhelming concern for Demi.

"I've tried it all. She just won't budge." Vincent rubbed his eyes to stifle the ever-present tears. "I'm worried about her."

"Don't worry, o gios mou, I'll pay her a visit tomorrow. Maybe she just needs a *real* mother to lift her spirits," she suggested.

"Yeah," Vincent replied. "That would mean a lot to her, I'm sure. I gotta go, Ma. I love you."

"I love you too. I'll come by tomorrow around three. Adío."

"Adío, Ma." Vincent hung up the phone and tossed it beside his notes. Trying to bring his focus back to the case at hand, he started from the beginning.

Alexander Travis' body had been found behind a convenience store beside a dumpster at the intersection of Cutt and Center on December 12, 2013. It had been called in by an unidentified woman, presumably a scared bystander quick to leave the scene, though no suspects could be ruled out.

The store clerk who worked that evening swore he saw no suspicious activity and did not recognize the luggage that the dismembered body was stuffed in. He quickly offered up the security camera tapes to aid officers, but the only camera outside facing the phone booth was down and the other, out back, hadn't gotten a clear image of the drop-off site. One camera inside the store had caught a figure through the window at the phone booth around the time the call had been made to the 911 dispatcher. However, the image offered little to no detail about the person's identity.

The caller had been at the booth for less than three minutes before leaving without entering the store at all.

Alexander's body had been identified thanks to his wallet, which was in the back pocket of his neatly folded jeans, placed in the luggage along with his other articles of clothing and the rags police assumed had been used to clean up the scene of the crime. His identity was further confirmed by his dental records, based on what few teeth he had left.

The corpse had been carefully dismembered, likely using a filleting knife or standard cleaver. Shards of glass in the facial wound were quickly confirmed to be from a bottle of scotch based on the contents of his stomach. His nasal cavity was completely crushed, and his lungs contained several ounces of blood.

The cause of death was determined to be blunt force trauma and suffocation.

Alexander didn't belong to the Portland area, or the state of Maine, for that matter, having taken up residence in Buffalo, New York. According to close friends and relatives, he had no acquaintances in Maine. They speculated he might have been up there looking for work. He had recently been let go from his teaching job for inappropriate conduct with a coworker. The details surrounding his dismissal were muddy and—not wanting to be affiliated with the murder—the school was uncooperative when questioned.

Much like this school, the few others that had employed Alexander were reform schools or Catholic academies. St. Francis-Assisi Catholic Academy, Red Hawk Academy for Girls, Sacred Heart Catholic Academy, St. Joan's Juvenile Detention Center.

St. Joan's... Where have I heard that before?

Vincent opened a new tab on his web browser and searched for the school. When the website came up, it didn't ring any bells. He searched for Alexander's years on the faculty and found that he had been on staff from 2008 to 2011.

A thought came to mind. *Wasn't Demi at a reform school around this time?*

Vincent opened up the bookmarked tabs he had saved of articles pertaining to Demi's past. Up came the first article he had found about her parents' murder, but it revealed nothing. The next two pertained more to what had been uncovered about the Malkins and Demi's recovery in the hospital. However, at the very end, one offered the information he was looking for.

It read:

```
As for the troubled teen, Prudence Malkin, she
is expected to make a full recovery following
the gruesome car accident that nearly took her
life. She will be placed in St. Joan's
Juvenile Detention Center, where she can
receive the therapy she needs and continue her
education.
```

The article was dated January 2008.

Vincent leaned back into the couch, scratching his chin thoughtfully. A voice deep down told him there must be some kind of connection. Had she been acquainted with Alexander when he taught at St. Joan's, she would be the only person he definitively knew in the state of Maine. Utilizing the map on an open tab, set on the convenience store at Cutt and Center, Vincent typed in the address of Demi's old apartment building. When he clicked "search," the screen loaded for a moment. Then the pin moved less than an inch away from the convenience store.

His stomach went leaden.

It can't be.

He looked over at the closed bedroom door, his palms clammy. He didn't want to believe she had anything to do with Alexander's murder. And yet...

Vincent shook his head. "No. There's no way."

Remembering that he had the recording of the 911 call from that night, Vincent opened it, stuck in his earphones, and hit "play."

"911, what's your emergency?" said the dispatcher.

"I'm at the intersection of Cutts and Center." The woman's voice was grainy. He increased the volume and listened more intently. *"There's a suitcase with human remains inside by the dumpster."*

He rewound it and played it again. His eyes widened.

"We'll dispatch an officer to you," the dispatcher replied. *"What's your name and callback number in case we get disconnected?... Hello? Hello, ma'am?"*

Then the recording ended.

Demi... no.

What was he thinking? This didn't mean *she* had done it. Maybe it was just a fucked-up coincidence that she had found the body of someone she might have known. His eyes shot over to the bedroom door again.

Only one way to find out.

Vincent stood and walked into the room to find that Demi was not in bed. He looked toward the bathroom. The door was closed, the light was on, and steam rolled from beneath it. A bit of relief lightened the weight in his shoulders just a fraction, as he was glad to see she had finally gotten out of bed. Perhaps her lucidity would make this conversation easier.

Vincent sat on the bed and waited for her to exit the bathroom. He heard the water shut off and the sound of the shower curtain sliding open. A few minutes passed. When she emerged, steam swirled around and off her body as if she were emitting it. Wrapped in her silk robe, her hair in a towel, she walked out of the bathroom and spotted him instantly.

"Hello, Vincent," she said.

Her voice was wrong.

It was cool and even. Her body was deathly still.

Did she sense what he was about to ask?

Did she somehow know that he knew?

"Dem, we have to talk," Vincent said, then patted the bed beside him. "Please have a seat."

She quirked her brow, her hands at her sides as she methodically popped each finger with her thumbs.

Vincent sat straighter. "Please?"

She nodded and did as he asked, her movements stiff and guarded as she took a seat beside him.

He faced her now, desperately hoping he was wrong about all of it. "You know the cold case I've been working on?"

She nodded slowly, her unblinking eyes studying him.

"The victim, Alexander Travis... Did you know him?"

Her brow furrowed and she finally blinked. Looking down into her lap, where her hands were folded together, she replied, "I did."

"Do you know who might have killed him?"

Her gaze made its way back up to his. Her eyes were sad, like those of a child who had been caught with chocolate on her face. She whispered, "I do."

He sighed, still hoping beyond all reason she wasn't the one who did it. "Can you tell me what happened?"

Demi bit her bottom lip and glanced away, unable to look at him as she shared her story. “Soon after Mother and Father died, I was sent to St. Joan’s, a school for troubled girls like me. Mr. Travis was my math teacher. I was struggling with what I know now to be my affliction, but I didn’t know what it was at the time. I was indignant, obstinate. I was enraged, but above all I craved that feeling, that rush I got from killing. It—it made me feel so excited that I was terrified by what I might do.”

Vincent was stunned. He knew she felt the need to kill, but never had she admitted to liking it. He scratched the back of his neck to hide the grimace on his face.

“Then, one day, I was early to Mr. Travis’ class. My excitement morphed into something else entirely. Something he could plainly see in the way I was acting and how I spoke to him. He fucked me over his desk. He used me like so many other men before him had done. It wasn’t until I was a few years older that I realized this, the power dynamic. A power he held over me on a societal level that I was too stupid to see because of how powerful I felt for the very first time in my life. I thought because I initiated it that I had all the control. In reality, he did.” Her eyes shot over to Vincent. They were tired and heavy despite all the time she had spent in bed the last few days. Her emotional distress had taken a very apparent toll.

Vincent just sat and listened, urging her to go on.

“Nothing happened after that. I left St. Joan’s after receiving my diploma and went on to college. After graduation, I was living on my own in a completely different state. My inclination was burning a hole in my stomach when I opened my front door and there he stood.

Six years later. He found me and was ready to start back where *he* felt we left off. He confessed he had been watching me for some time before he *got up the courage* to come to my door. All my anger came rushing back when that man, that *rapist*, inserted himself back into my life without my consent. To him, I was a prize to reclaim. I got him drunk so he'd let his guard down. Then I bashed his face in with the butt of the liquor bottle until it was broken and he was dead."

Vincent was quiet. Disbelief and frustration played a tug of war in his gut. She stared at him, wanting him to say something, wanting him to comfort her and tell her it was alright. But it wasn't.

"Why didn't you go to the police and report him for stalking?" he finally asked.

She scoffed. "Report him for stalking? Do you have any idea how often women report men for stalking only to not be taken seriously and wind up dead anyway? Restraining orders and the police do nothing to protect women from deranged men who believe them to be their property unless that man has killed them already. Do you even have a clue about the statistics surrounding cases of abused and murdered women who report their stalkers only to be told that there is nothing law enforcement can do for them unless they are in immediate danger? Negating the fact that she is in immediate danger every *fucking* second her stalker is out there!"

"I'm not trying to diminish what you had to have been dealing with, but Dem..." Vincent shook his head, his agitation rising. "You can't just kill people because you see fit. You are not judge, jury, and executioner!"

"No, I am GOD!" she screamed, rising to her feet and standing over him with a crazed look in her eyes. "I choose who can and can't be in my life, and if I am wronged, they *will* pay! I told myself fourteen years ago that no one else would go unpunished for the things they did to hurt me. No one!"

"Demi, you have to know that that's not ok," he pleaded, reaching for her hand.

She slapped his hand away. "Stop calling me that! Demi died the day Justine put me in Lara's arms."

Had he been wrong for referring to her only as Demi all this time? Was he inadvertently holding her to a standard she did not confidently think she could live up to? "That doesn't mean that you aren't *good*! You are good regardless of the name you choose to use."

"I'll be a good girl in hell," Demi growled, then stormed back into the bathroom, shutting and locking the door behind her. "Get out!"

Vincent's face fell in his hands. It took everything in him to keep from tearing down the bathroom door and pleading with her to tell him none of this was true. He couldn't turn her in for this, couldn't admit to the CID what he had uncovered. She'd never see the light of day after that, no matter what bargain Seifert offered her.

He didn't know what to do.

Chapter 23

Vincent didn't leave the room.

Not all night, anyway.

He gave Prudence time to calm down before returning with a bowl of soup and toasted bread for dinner. For the first time in five days, she ate. The warm broth satiated the hunger she had been combating, and the bread filled her belly. She finally drank the cup of water that sat by the bed and even went to the kitchen for a second glass. She thanked him for the soup, but they did not speak for the remainder of the evening.

What was there to say?

He was likely contemplating whether to turn her in for Alexander's murder. She wouldn't blame him. It *was* his job, after all. She only wished he could see it the way she did, see it for the necessity that it was. But she wasn't in the business of changing minds, nor did she want to try and change Vincent's. One of the things she appreciated about Vincent was his dedication to the truth. Attempting to change his morals would be akin to changing the fundamentals of who he was.

Her anger was far outshined by her adoration for him.

Vincent fell asleep in the bed beside her after walking Broccoli one last time for the night. Prudence lay there wide awake with nothing but Ramona on her mind. The truth was maddening, practically impossible to come to terms with. The mother she had longed for, the mother she had never known existed, was the same person who had subjected her to a life of pain and suffering.

Her puzzle was finally complete and she couldn't stand the sight of it.

After hours of tossing and turning, Prudence quietly slid out of bed and put on some clothes and shoes. Looking at Vincent to ensure she had not woken him, she was struck by his handsome sleeping face. He lay facing her side of the bed, his arms stretched out, seeming to reach for her. His features were soft except for a slight crinkle between his brows. The faint voice of reason in her head told her to lie back down and curl into him. It told her that solace would be found in his arms and she need not do what she was planning on doing. It told her that Vincent was all she really needed.

But will he be able to let go of the fact that I killed Alex?

Will he keep my secret and not turn me in?

No, he wouldn't be able to live with himself.

What does one more body matter, anyway?

With a heavy heart, she left the room.

In the living room, she spotted the laptop and Vincent's notebooks on the coffee table. After opening the computer, she logged in to find a slew of emails from Andres and Dr. Agubulom, none of which she opened and read. Instead, she brought up the directions to the Callards' house in Glassboro, New Jersey. Using a blank page from one of Vincent's notebooks, she wrote down the directions, tore the page out, and grabbed the keys to his truck.

Prudence had stopped by the front door to slip on her jacket when Broccoli jumped up, his paws reaching up against her legs. She looked down into his large, bulging eyes as he groaned and huffed at her. She scratched the sweet spots between his ears and under his chin.

"Goodbye, Broccoli," she whispered to the pup. "Thank you for being such a good boy."

Prudence kissed the dog on the head and left the apartment.

◆

The miles passed like inches, the hours like minutes, as Prudence drove Vincent's truck through the night back to her parents' house.

Back to Ramona.

All the while, she contemplated how she would do it. Would she use the familiar blade of a kitchen knife? Perhaps she would strangle Ramona with her bare hands. Maybe she would tie her to a chair and beat her over the head with that fucking Pyrex dish of hers. Sever each finger and toe, then her hands, then her feet. She'd work her way up until all that was left was her head—if she didn't die from shock before then.

Whatever Prudence chose to do, it would not be quick and it would not be painless.

In fact, she planned on drawing it out as long as humanly possible. That woman deserved far worse than any of the others she had killed. Worse than Alex and Benitez, worse than those heinous bitches in solitary. Even worse than Mother and Father, the perpetrators of her abuse.

Prudence pulled into their driveway. It was close to four in the morning. The sky was still shadowed by night and all the lights in the house appeared to be off. She got out of the truck, headed straight for the door, and pounded her fists against it.

"Justine!" Prudence yelled. "Justine! It's your little girl!"

She banged with the full force of her body. Her limbs shook, still weak from malnourishment, but her rage fueled her enough to carry on. She would kill this woman if it took everything she had left inside.

"Open up!"

She heard the door being unlocked. It swung open to reveal Andres. His expression was melancholy, his eyes tired when they fell on her.

Prudence pushed past him and into the house. "Where is she?"

He shut the door and followed her. "She isn't here."

Prudence charged down the hall, opening every door and turning on every light. "Don't lie to me! Where is she?"

She looked in every room, inside every closet, behind every curtain, but Ramona wasn't there. Andres stood in the hall and waited for her to come out of the spare bedroom—the room he had promised she and Vincent could stay in several days ago.

Prudence emerged panting and shaking. Her adrenaline was depleting rapidly. "Where *is* she?" she cried, feeling desperate, utterly and painfully hopeless. Her chest ached and her stomach burned. This was not how she typically felt when she was moments away from taking someone's life. She always felt excited, weightless, like dancing to her favorite tune as the music swelled in her bosom and stimulated her senses.

Right now, she felt haggard and exhausted. Most of all, her insides felt completely depthless, like a series of caves going underground for hundreds of miles. She reached within, but there was no bottom to touch. There was nothing but endless troves of heartache and agony.

Andres sniffed, wiping away the tears that coated his cheeks as he struggled to look at his daughter. "She isn't here, Demi."

Prudence swayed from side to side, finding it difficult to stay standing. She couldn't summon another scream, couldn't hardly summon the energy to speak. "Wh—where... Where is she?"

"I don't know where she is," he admitted, throwing his hands up in defeat. His white flag was raised on a flimsy stick. "I tried to confront her after you both left, but she packed a bag and left too. I've been alone in this house for days. Nobody picking up the phone when I call. I would put out a missing persons report for her, but I don't want them bringing her back to me. She belongs in jail."

"Just like me," Prudence replied. Her legs were so weak that her knees buckled and she crumpled to the floor. Andres reached for her and held her up as best as he could, then helped her to the dining room table. He sat her down and left her there while he put on a pot of coffee. When he returned, he had the pot and a cup for both of them.

"You take cream and sugar?" Andres asked.

She nodded in response.

Andres went back in the kitchen and returned with a carton of cream, a bowl of sugar, and a large muffin. He spooned some sugar into both mugs, then a bit of cream. He stirred hers first and then his.

"Drink up now. Vincent told me that you hadn't been eating. Must be completely out of sorts," Andres instructed, sipping his coffee and clearing his throat.

Prudence's brow furrowed and her eyes shot over to him. "You spoke to Vincent."

"Yes. He called me around midnight. Said you were gone, along with his truck. He was worried you would come here and he wanted to give me a heads up." He handed her the muffin. "You've got yourself a good man, sweetie."

She took the pastry and set it down, choosing to just sip her coffee for now. "He deserves better than me."

"Don't say that," he said, shaking his head.

"I've killed people, Andres. I've spent time in prison and I'm out now only because—"

He held his hand up to stop her. "You were dealt a shitty hand and have had to make some difficult choices—choices most people are never forced to make. I don't know everything you've done and I don't need to know because you're my daughter. I lost you once. I will not lose you again."

Tears swelled in her eyes and Prudence's face contorted as a sob took over. She cupped her face in her hand and heaved, unable to control herself. Andres rose and wrapped his arms around her, rubbing her back gently.

"It's ok, sweetie. Dad is here," he said, hiccupping on his own tears. It must have been so bittersweet to finally be in the presence of his daughter only to lose his wife in the process. Prudence understood so well exactly what he was feeling. She held him tightly, her tears soaking his shirt, doing her best to calm down.

"Hey, do you want to know something?" Andres asked, pulling away from her and taking her hands into his as he sat back down.

She sniffed. "Sure."

"When you were born, I would sing to you every day. I sang a song called 'Baby I Love You' by a musician you've probably never heard of, Andy Kim. Anyway, instead of 'baby,' I'd sing 'Demi.'"

Prudence listened intently as he started singing his rendition to her. Despite their trembling, her lips curled into a slight smile as his voice carried the tune. A song to cheer her up. A song to soothe her pain. A song just for her.

"*Demi, I love you... Demi, I love you.*"

Prudence cried and laughed and cried some more. "You really did love me, didn't you, Dad?" The word rolled off her tongue in an unfamiliar but delightful way.

He smiled, a low chuckle in his chest. "More than anything," he replied. "I always tell people that you saved my life the day you were born. Before you and your brother, I had nothing to live for. I was selfish and wasn't worried about anyone or anything. But when you two were born? Well, I had to get my shit together!" Andres squeezed her hand gently, his voice growing sad. "And the day you were taken from me, I knew I'd never stop looking. Never. Even if, when I did finally find you, I could see you for only an hour. Knowing you were ok would be enough for me." He kissed her hand before releasing it. "Now drink up and eat that muffin. You look like you're about to blow away."

Prudence laughed and did as her father said. She sipped her coffee, then picked up the muffin and sank her teeth into it. Banana nut.

Aside from time spent with Vincent, nothing felt as serene as this moment, sipping coffee and eating a muffin with her father. She watched him adoringly as he fixed her a second cup and dabbed her mouth with a napkin to rid her face of crumbs. She didn't want to lose him again either.

"Dad?"

His eyes lit up. "Yeah, sweetie?"

"Have you thought about what happens next?" she began, clutching her mug tightly and tapping her nails on its ceramic side. "With Justine?"

He shook his head. "I've tried not thinking about it at all, to tell you the truth."

"And if she comes back?" Prudence sipped her coffee.

Andres sighed, his fingers tapping the wooden tabletop, "Then the police will be waiting for her."

Prudence liked that idea. Let the police handle her. She was done playing vigilante. Her hands were eternally stained with enough blood.

She finished her muffin and second cup of coffee, feeling better than before, but still terribly drained. "Dad?"

"Yeah, sweetie?"

"You think I could sleep here a while before I head back to Portland?" she asked.

"You thought I was gonna let you hit the road without getting some rest? What kind of father do you take me for?" He winked, his voice carrying on a laugh.

Prudence smiled and excused herself to the spare bedroom, where she slept the day away.

CHAPTER 24

December 2007

Dirt and grime laced the carpet beneath Lara's feet. She was seated in front of the motel room where Prue was inside with a client. She and Sam took turns doing so to ensure no John took off without paying or got too rough with the girl.

She was no good to them dead.

Much like the other motels they frequented, this one was filthy and had a stench imbued with mold that wafted through the drafty halls. Lara hated these places but had agreed a long time ago that it was way better than having the men come to their home. The neighbors were nosey, especially the lesbians next door, Joy and Emma. On several occasions over the years, they had tried to talk to Prue and even went so far as to invite them over for their holiday functions.

Fourteen years later and they still hadn't gotten the hint.

At least here at the motel the clerk never asked questions and the other guests kept to themselves, no matter what horrific sounds came from the room when Prue was servicing a client. Though the last few years, no sounds—aside from the repugnant groaning of whichever man was with her—traveled past the door. A small part of Lara was grateful for that because Prue's screams and cries for her "mother" and "father" had started wearing her down. Though she refused to open up her heart and allow herself to be an actual mother to Prue, as time went on, guilt began to set in, growing like a weed in her mind year after year. She had hoped her indifference would keep her from looking at the girl as human, which, in turn, would make what they subjected her to easier.

At first, Lara had been consumed by her jealousy of Prue over all the attention and love she got from Sam. He was *Lara's*, after all, and she didn't want any woman—or girl—taking him from her. As a child herself at the time, it was too easy to be blinded by all that was so terribly wrong about what was happening. As Prue got older, Lara noticed that Sam's affections gradually shifted to the child. It had begun when Prue was around seven or eight. He had started sleeping a few nights a week in her room as opposed to sleeping in the room he and Lara shared. When Prue turned ten, Lara noticed the way he started speaking to her.

It was a lot like how he had spoken to Lara when they had first met.

He had told Prue how mature she was, how sexy and intelligent she was. Sam had begun making moves on the girl as well, but by eleven, she was changing too. Prue didn't search for their affection anymore. Instead, she isolated herself in her room every second she could to read her books. Her tone when she spoke was curt and her eyes grew vicious and filled with hate. Not that Lara could blame her.

At this point, she hated herself too.

The door swung open and the John stepped out, still fastening his belt like the giant pig he was. Lara's lip hiked up in a snarl as she stood, swiped the bills from his hand, and stuffed them in her pocket.

When she entered the room, Prue was already in the shower, steam rolling out from beneath the bathroom door. The girl ran it so hot sometimes that she'd come out with welts and blisters on her skin. Though Lara knew she was likely in pain, she didn't cry anymore.

Not a single tear.

She didn't express any emotion at all, for that matter. Prue had likely learned this from her, as Lara, too, had become an impenetrable carapace that not a soul could persuade to share her hand. The only difference was that Lara's shell was wearing very thin and Prue's seemed to be getting thicker every day.

The water shut off and Prue exited the bathroom wearing the fresh clothes that she had learned to pack for herself in the event that the John dirtied or ruined the ones she initially wore.

"Let's go. Your father is waiting outside," Lara instructed, walking back out of the room. Prue dutifully scooped up her backpack and walked a few paces behind Lara out of the motel and to the car. Sam was parked with the car running to keep warm just outside the front door. Lara and Prue climbed inside, the cold air biting their ankles as they did.

"How are my two favorite ladies!" Sam said as they buckled their seatbelts. Neither of them answered.

Not that he actually cares, Lara thought.

He drove out of the parking lot and onto the highway toward the house. This was one of the farthest-away motels they frequented, and it would take them around an hour to get home, even with light traffic.

The sky was pitch black and snowflakes appeared in the headlight beams. The roads were slick and icy.

It would be a white Christmas after all.

Christmases at the Malkin household were nonexistent, as Sam had been raised a Jehovah's Witness, but Lara deeply missed what it meant to celebrate every year. She remembered how her aunts and uncles and cousins came into town the week of Christmas and stayed at their house with her parents, her sister, and her.

They'd go ice skating, bake cookies, and watch Christmas movies every night leading up until Christmas day with cups of cocoa or hot apple cider. Her mother would buy the entire family matching pajamas that they'd wear on Christmas Eve for their annual photo in front of the tree. The tree was never shorter than seven feet and was drenched in ornaments, ropes of strung popcorn, and silver tinsel. Every surface in the house was covered with decorations: porcelain Santas, miniature nativity scenes, wooden elves, and nutcrackers. Shoved on every bare space was a cottony fluff that somewhat resembled snow and that was riddled with glitter. The sparkly substance coated the floor and, by the end of the season, ended up in every corner of the house.

Lara missed those days, missed her family.

She hadn't been allowed to see them since she had run away with Sam eighteen years ago. Sam who had taken her virtue. Sam who controlled her entire life. Sam who hadn't fucked her in nearly seven years.

Sam who took everything and gave nothing in return.

Lara shook her head, released a heavy breath, and lit a cigarette. She rolled the window down just enough for the smoke to escape and puffed on the cig until it was done. She lit another, pulling on it just as fast. Once her nerves were satiated, she pulled from her pocket the crumpled bills that the John had given her and counted them.

One hundred and forty dollars. The girl was worth $140 a pop to that goddamn slob and Sam fucking agreed to it.

Lara clenched the bills in her fist and looked up at the rearview mirror. Prue sat there, her head down, her face vacant. It was what she looked like every waking moment.

Lara's chest tightened and she looked away.

"It's not enough," she said. Her voice was so loud in the quiet car that she flinched.

"What? Did that fuck not give you the whole $140?" Sam asked, immediately irate.

"No, Sam. One hundred and forty dollars isn't enough. We can't continue doing this to Pru—"

A sharp pain erupted through her head.

Hot liquid poured from her eye and down her cheek.

Lara's vision was spotted and blurred.

The image of Christmas lights twinkled in her mind, then faded to black.

CHAPTER 25

June 2020

It was late that night when Prudence made it home, and Vincent was still up waiting for her. Andres had told her he'd let Vincent know that she was headed home, so the fact that he'd stayed up came as no surprise, but her heart fluttered to life just the same. The moment she opened the door, Vincent leaped from the couch and picked her up, crushing her body against his. Kissing along her cheek and neck, he asked her repeatedly if she was alright.

"I'm fine, Vincent. I'm fine, I promise," she assured him until he finally set her back down on her feet, though he still held her close. He searched her face for anything amiss, but there was nothing to find.

She was truly and utterly content.

The time spent with Andres, and the long trip there and back, had put a lot of things into perspective for her. Everything had finally clicked into place and she was able to find clarity with who she was and what she really and truly needed.

"I'm so sorry, Dem. I'm sorry for upsetting you last night. I promise I do understand why you—"

She raised her hand to stop him, just as her father had done with her hours before. "Don't apologize. I know you, Officer Kore. You are an honorable man who is just in your beliefs. You stick firmly to your moral code, something I have never quite been able to conform to, especially when it came to what I perceived to be my own best interest. But I wouldn't change this aspect of you no matter how ferocious the disagreement."

"I won't turn you in, Demi," Vincent proclaimed, his hands squeezing her waist. "Once tomorrow is done and over with, nothing will take you from me. Especially not a dead creep like Alexander Travis."

Prudence searched his eyes, her hands on his chest, reveling in the sheer love that swam in them. Heat bloomed within her chest and spread throughout her core.

"Make love to me, Vincent," she said, pressing her hips into his, her desire for him taking the reins.

Vincent kissed her sweetly. "Say it again."

Prudence fisted his shirt and stood on her tiptoes, brushing her lips over his. "Make love to me," she repeated before kissing him so fiercely that she knocked the wind out of his lungs.

Vincent made love to her that night until they were both satiated and seeing stars in the pitch-black ceiling of their bedroom.

◆

The courtroom was cold and virtually empty, Vincent noticed, as he looked around him. He was the sole occupant of the first row of benches in the gallery. Standing at a podium a few feet in front of him, with only a bar separating them, was Demi, surrounded by a transparent plastic barrier. She looked so beautiful and statuesque in a gray pencil skirt, a white long-sleeved blouse, and nude heels. Her curls were wound up in a bun at the top of her crown, with stray curls here and there about her face. The way she stood so poised and confident quelled his jittery nerves. Vincent was in awe of her ability to remain calm. Meanwhile, he couldn't decide whether he was excited or terrified.

Excited for this to be over and to start their lives together anew.

Terrified that the judge wouldn't believe their lies.

The honorable Judge Robinson entered the courtroom and walked up to the bench, which was surrounded by a similar transparent barrier. The few other people in the courtroom rose as she came. Then they sat when instructed to do so by the officer of the court. Everyone sat appropriately distanced from one another, wearing face masks, including Warden Seifert, who stood off to the side, monitoring Demi closely. They had spent a good deal of time going over their story and how they would present their case to the judge.

Several minutes earlier, Seifert had been exactly where Demi stood, giving his account of events from the night Benitez and the other inmates were murdered. He had explained what he wanted Judge Robinson to believe was true. That Benitez went on a murdering spree, likely due to the drugs that had been found in his system post-mortem. It was well known that Benitez took and sold drugs, so this notion wasn't far-fetched, but even Vincent had to admit that it was a bit of a stretch to believe someone mildly high on cocaine could have done, on a whim, what Demi had done.

He saw the pictures of the scenes left behind in each cell. He remembered the blood that spilled from those women's bodies and coated the floor. Their heads brutally mutilated, their chests caved in.

Some were missing teeth, their jaws torn out of place. It was like a wild bear had been unleashed upon them.

A beast of grand proportions.

That's not who she is anymore, Vincent told himself, looking at her now.

"Good afternoon, Ms. Prudence Malkin," Judge Robinson began. "Thank you for joining us today to provide your witness statement in regard to the deaths of Flor Juarez, Anita Bell, Elanor Johnson, Mari Velasco, and Edgar Benitez."

"It's Demi."

Vincent blinked, shocked by her correction of the judge and yet elated.

Judge Robinson did not appear to be impressed. She furrowed her brow and leaned forward in her seat. "Excuse me?"

"Due to recent findings about my having been kidnapped as a child, it has been determined via paternity test that my name is not, in fact, Prudence Malkin. My legal birth name is Demi Callard and I would very much like to be referred to by that name," Demi explained. She was as stoic as she had ever been, her unwavering focus ahead.

"I am sorry to hear about what happened to you, but according to the state of Maine, you are still Prudence Malkin. I suggest you take it up with the Social Security office when we are through." Judge Robinson paused, seeming to consider her next words. "However, I will respect your wishes, Ms. Callard."

"Thank you, your honor." Demi bowed her head, then peered over her shoulder at Vincent, who beamed with pride at her choice to use her real name.

The name of the girl stolen.

The name of the girl thrust into the dark.

The name of the girl who would soon be set free.

"If you would, please, inform the court of what you witnessed that night," the judge instructed.

Vincent adjusted in his seat and leaned forward, resting his elbows on his knees. His suit jacket, which he admittedly did not wear often, was snug on his ample shoulders. He watched Demi's hands at her sides as she popped each finger with her thumbs, her nerves present now.

You have nothing to be nervous about, baby, Vincent thought, wishing he could say it to her out loud. *Just remember what Seifert told you to say.*

She took a deep breath, smoothed down the front of her skirt, and began. "Benitez was late coming in for his shift that night. It must have been forty-five minutes past seven. He came in and, in his usual fashion, started to rile up the inmates—myself in particular. Edgar and I had had an encounter before my incarceration, and when I rejected his advances upon entering the prison, he did not take it very well."

Vincent noticed her look over toward Seifert briefly, then back at the judge as she continued.

That's right, baby, you've got this.

"He was terrorizing me. The other inmates became excited by his taunting and proceeded to cheer him on. Feeling I had no choice but to accept his advances, I seduced him into my cell. Edgar came inside, he grabbed me... I—I couldn't let him have me... I couldn't let anyone have me in that way again."

Vincent's brows crossed. This was not the version of events they had discussed. His gaze shot over to Seifert, who crossed his arms as he stared at Demi with eyes ablaze. Vincent exhaled, rubbing his clammy hands together, and concluded that she had just misspoken. He was sure she'd get back on course.

"There was a scuffle. Then I managed to get his baton away from him and I—I murdered him with it."

Judge Robinson was at the edge of her seat, her elbows on the bench, confusion lacing her expression. "If that's so, Ms. Callard, when exactly did Officer Benitez kill the other inmates?"

Vincent gripped the partition in front of him, watching Demi from behind. He could see her hands at her sides trembling.

"Edgar Benitez did not kill them, your honor. I did."

Vincent felt sick as shock eroded the lining of his stomach. Murmurs spread throughout the courtroom, like a swarm of wasps buzzing around them. He had to stop her, had to make her realize that she had misspoken. Vincent stood, leaned toward her, and said, "Demi, what are you doing?"

Her head bowed and her shoulders shot up to her ears like she was trying to tune everyone out. She did not acknowledge him, did not try to backtrack on what she had just admitted. Vincent turned to Seifert, who wore a look of utter bewilderment, his crossed arms coming unfurled.

"I killed them all, sparing inmate Collins. I would also like to add that I am responsible for the 2013 murder of Alexander Travis, whose case remains unsolved. I am prepared to pay the price for what *I* have done." Her shoulders dropped and she looked over at Seifert.

"Not a dead man that the prison chose to ignore despite his transgressions with the inmates."

Seifert's face was beet red as he waved his arms and stepped forward from his place against the wall. "Your honor! She's lying! This is not what she told us!"

Vincent jumped over the partition, ready to stand between the warden and Demi, when an officer stopped Seifert in his tracks and gave Vincent a warning glare to get back to his seat. But Vincent did no such thing. He just stood there within arm's reach of Demi.

"Is that so?" Judge Robinson snapped, banging her gavel. "Then perhaps you can produce the video evidence to prove it, Warden Seifert."

The warden went white as a sheet. Vincent knew that all video evidence had been intentionally lost. The Judge was unconvinced that it did not exist and it was obviously clear to her now why that is. Seifert's eyes wide, he stuttered as he tried to plead with her. The buzzing in the room intensified as Judge Robinson slammed her gavel again to regain order. However, Vincent couldn't worry about all that. Not when his girl had just thrown her entire life away.

The life the two of them were meant to share.

He gazed at her in front of him. She was still standing there as if the room wasn't up in arms around her. As if there wasn't a huge crack in the Earth where she had just fractured it. Vincent removed his mask, his chest tight, and said, "Dem?"

Demi turned around, her face unreadable.

"Baby, what are you doing?" he asked. His anguish had him in a chokehold.

"I couldn't lie, Vincent," she whispered, removing her mask. Her chin trembled. "I can't keep running from the consequences of my actions and allowing you to sacrifice everything you stand for just to be with me."

Vincent could hardly breathe. "But what about us?"

He heard Seifert raging somewhere off to the side, with the judge threatening him with contempt of court, but none of it mattered.

"You wouldn't have been able to live with yourself if you didn't turn me in for what I did to Alex. It's just not who you are," she replied, tears lining her eyes. "And I can't expect that of you."

Vincent took her hands in his, holding them to his chest. "No, no, I said I wouldn't. Your being with me means more than solving that fucking case. You have to know that."

His heart broke when she tried to pull away. "I should be in jail, Vincent... I'm a murderer."

"But you've changed!" he objected, squeezing her hands, the fear of knowing she would soon be taken from him causing him to panic. "You didn't kill Justine. You're getting better, I can see it! I know it!"

Despite the blood rushing through his ears as his heart pounded away in his chest, Vincent could hear Judge Robinson say, "You have been found in contempt, Warden Seifert! Remove him from my court and arrest Ms. Callard for the murders of Flor Juarez, Anita Bell, Elanor—"

Her voice faded as all his attention went to Demi's hands, shaking between his. She was struggling to hold herself together. Vincent's breaths came in sharp pants. The room was closing in as he saw another officer near them out of the corner of his eye.

"You don't understand!" Demi cried. "If she had been home, I *would* have killed her. I'm where I need to be and you—you shouldn't have to deal with any of this."

"No, I can't expect that. I won't!" Vincent replied, frantically pulling her closer with the full force of his being.

Demi shook her head, her inner turmoil ripping her to pieces. "I refuse to allow our love to be tainted by lies and deceit, Vincent."

The officer closed in on them and grabbed her by the arm, ripping her from Vincent's hold. He fumbled to grab her again, but she was held back, her hands cuffed.

"Let go of her!" Vincent yelled, charging at them. The officer ordered him to stay away, but he refused to listen as he took hold of her and tried to pry her away.

"I—I," her voice cracked as she started to cry. "I love you, Vincent. With all that I am, I love you."

Vincent froze, disbelief rendering him immobile. Tears welled up and cascaded down his face. "I love you too, Dem."

"Then please... Please let me love you in the best way that I can." She wept, her chest heaving, unable to take in air. "Please. You have to let me go."

In a single swift motion, she leaned in and kissed him for the last time. Savoring the feel of his lips, the smell of his skin, the tickle of his beard. He was hers and she was his, even if only for one second more.

For Vincent, everything around them faded in that second. His mind, body, and soul were waging a war within to prevent the tether connecting their hearts from ripping and tearing apart. His mangled heart struggled to beat within his chest. Pieces of it flaked away as it held fast to the tether.

"Goodbye," she whispered against his lips. Then time sped up and, in the blink of an eye, she was torn away.

"No, no, please, Demi!" Vincent yelled. Someone grabbed him from behind, then another, both trying to hold him back as she was taken from him.

Slamming her gavel again, Judge Robinson said, "Mr. Kore! Stand down before you too find yourself in cuffs!"

Demi disappeared behind a door to the left of the judge's bench. Only then did he stop resisting, incredulously staring at the closed door.

She was gone.

The tether snapped.

◗

Demi was led out of the courtroom. When the door closed on Vincent's face, she fell apart. Her legs gave out and she wilted in the arms of the officer who had dragged her away, unable to stand.

She had decided, during the long drive back from her father's home the night before, that she would not be like her mother. She would not run away from what she had done. She was better than that, so much stronger than that. She would face the consequences head-on, even if it killed her to do so.

Even if it meant losing the man she loved.

Her soul dripped with gratitude for his love. She felt it in the very marrow of her bones even now, the ghost of his kiss still fresh on her lips. Vincent devotedly submerged her in love's extravagance, bathed her in its restorative waters, and brought her back to life.

He brought her back to herself.

She would love him until the day she died and then for an eternity more.

Demi regained her equilibrium, the thought of Vincent's love stabilizing her, and the officer helping her to her feet. She blinked away the last of her tears, straightened her spine, lifted her head high, and pulled her shoulders back. She continued their walk down the hall with the conviction of having done the right thing, humming the song that her true father had sung especially for her.

ACKNOWLEDGEMENTS

If you have made it this far I would first like to thank you with all of my heart for not only taking a chance on my work, but for seeing it through to the very end. My books mean the world to me and it's people like you that make this whole crazy roller coaster of a process worth while.

Next I would like to thank Kim, my bonus mom and highly regarded friend. Kim, I dedicated this book to you because of your unwavering support and love. You were amongst the first I ever shared my silly little stories with at the young age of twelve. And when I learned that you actually read them, even printed them out to file away in a special binder with my name on it, I felt more special than I had ever felt in my life. You have, in real time, watched my writing grow and evolve from incoherent—yet charming—nonsense into what it is today. Finally you have been a constant source of motivation for me to keep writing and I couldn't be more grateful for you. I love you to the moon and back.

I would also like to thank my father James, whom I pulled a great deal of inspiration from when writing the character, Andres Callard. You're an immensely talented artist and musician who has molded me into the intelligent and dark humored individual I am today. Thank you for hyping up my books to every person you meet, thank you for loving me and my work even if the more adult themes aren't your thing. Thank you for your support and encouragement. Daddy, I love you.

Thank you to my best friend Donna Willis. You are not only a sensational, loving, and genuine friend, but you have supported me in my writing since I told you about my aspirations to publish my work. As someone who is as intelligent and thoughtful as you, your input is so valuable to me. You are always amongst the first to share what I have coming up and have introduced my work to people it likely would have never reached without your help. I love you lots.

Thank you to my husband Jeremiah. You inspire me, you push me, you support me and you sit and listen to my endless rantings when I'm trying to audibly work through my ideas in order to make any sense out of them. You help keep me sane when my mind gets dark and too filled with thicket keeping me from seeing the light. You are my sunshine, my bullfrog, meine erdbeere, and I love you so much.

Finally I want to thank my editor Tonya Bluston, my family and friends who support me, the masterminds behind the Atticus formatting system and Ingram Spark, my darling sons, and every single indie author out there making their dreams come true and inspiring people like me to do the same.

www.ingramcontent.com/pod-product-compliance
Lightning Source LLC
LaVergne TN
LVHW010546160826
845677LV00013B/3025